THE FIRE STAR

A MAVEN & REEVE MYSTERY

the Fire Star

A MAVEN & REEVE MYSTERY

A. L. TAIT

Kane Miller
A DIVISION OF EDC PUBLISHING

First American Edition 2022
Kane Miller, A Division of EDC Publishing

First published by Penguin Random House Australia Pty Ltd.
This edition published by arrangement with
Penguin Random House Australia Pty Ltd.
The Fire Star © A. L. Tait, 2020
The moral right of the author has been asserted.

For information contact:
Kane Miller, A Division of EDC Publishing
5402 S 122nd E Ave
Tulsa, OK 74146
www.kanemiller.com
www.myubam.com

Library of Congress Control Number: 2021944817

Printed and bound in the United States of America
1 2022
ISBN: 978-1-68464-437-7

For my own Beech Circle,
you know who you are.

CHAPTER ONE

Wednesday

Of all the things I'd imagined might stop us from reaching Rennart Castle by nightfall, goats had not even made the top fifty.

Before setting out, my number one source of nightmares had been that we'd encounter the King's men. But four horsemen wearing King Bren's gold-embroidered tunics had galloped past us a few miles back, flinging nothing more than mud and disdain in our direction as they'd carelessly forced us off the narrow road.

Once they'd rounded the bend toward the capital, I'd breathed a sigh of relief, thinking our passage clear.

After all, if the loathed King's disreputable followers had left us alone, then surely nothing would stop us?

And yet, here we are, minutes later, held hostage by six goats, a lame horse and an overturned cart.

And the boy. Wearing the tunic emblazoned with the bright-blue fox that marks him as property of Sir Garrick Sharp, Knight Protector of Rennart Castle, he is my lady's worst nightmare come to life in black hose and tall black boots. I'd heard her utter a most unladylike word under her breath as we'd rounded the corner at full canter, nearly taking out a hairy white goat before skidding to a stop.

"All hail," the boy had shouted, red-faced as he'd wrestled an unhappy brown goat toward a wooden crate lying on its side by the cart. "Sorry, good mistresses. Won't be a jiffy. Just helping Master Seymour here with his goats. He, er, ran into some trouble."

"Trouble ran into me, more like," the old man had muttered. "That young wastrel's lackeys, intent only on themselves, as usual."

I did not look at Cassandra, and neither of us had replied. Whispers about King Bren and his friends and their pleasure-seeking, lawbreaking ways waft across the kingdom of Cartreff on every breeze, but it would not do to discuss them here, on the road, with strangers. People have been hanged for less.

After watching the boy for a few moments, I begin to

realize that "a jiffy" might last a very long time if we have to rely on the goat-herding skills of this squire. Having finally grabbed hold of the brown goat with one hand, he tries to right the overturned crate with the other before realizing he needs two hands . . . and lets go of the goat.

With a quiet oath, he pushes the crate upright before setting off after the goat again but, every time he moves, the goats scatter in different directions, bleating with indignation.

I risk a glance at Cassandra, but she has pulled the hood of her tattered cloak down low and is unrecognizable within its folds. Her hand taps her cloak, right where the saddlebag would be, as it has done hundreds of times since we left home. She knows it is secure, its contents wrapped safely inside, but she cannot help herself — as I could not, were I in her position.

I turn my attention back to the boy, who is so busy with his goat duties he barely glances our way, giving me ample time to observe him. When they'd handed out looks, this boy had been front and center, waving his arms and flashing a charming smile. From his perfect blond ringlets to his dimple, he is what my sisters would describe as worth watching.

When they'd handed out brains, however . . .

"You do realize that's not going to work, don't you?" I say at last, taking care to use the harsh vowels of a peasant girl.

Cassandra flashes me a hard stare, but we do not have time to waste watching this boy flail about in the dust while a dazed old man looks on.

"What do you mean?" the boy asks, flushing an even deeper red.

"You can't talk them into the crate," I say. "They're not young ladies to be charmed. And even if they were, you'd need to do better than that. Polite chiding will not herd goats."

I cannot resist the dig. I may be only fifteen, but I have seen his type before, over and over. Dark-haired, blond, redheaded, it doesn't matter. They are always charming, always affecting the latest fashion in tunics or poetry or swordplay and always, in the end, utterly useless at anything beyond flowery words.

"Humph," the boy says. "If you know so much about goats, you do better." His lapse of courtly manners shows me just how fed up he is. Squires like him are usually on their best behavior at all times – in public, anyway.

"No –" I hear Cassandra begin, but I have already slithered off the horse and landed square on the road. Mother always said that my inability to resist a challenge would one day be my downfall. Then again, Mother always said a lot of things.

"Oh, fine then," Cassandra continues. "But make it snappy. We do have better places to be."

My challenger has moved to sit next to the silent old

4

man on the edge of the overturned cart and is now waving in the direction of the goats as though to say "have at it."

"The key," I say, moving purposefully toward the largest goat, a sizeable nanny with a full white beard, "is to show them who is boss."

"Is that so?" says the boy as the old man passes him an apple. He has regained some of his poise, and I give him points for that. His tunic appears new, which surprises me, as he looks to be at least sixteen. That blue fox should have a few years' wear on it by now, as most squires take up their duties by the age of fourteen.

"Indeed," I respond, even as my mind works through the conundrum of his background. "One must establish oneself as the leader of the herd."

I hear a loud crunch behind me and realize that the boy is munching his apple. But I remain fixed on the nanny goat as I approach, looking deep into her sharp brown eyes. I stand over her for a few moments, making sure I have her complete attention, before I turn and begin walking slowly toward the crate.

To my absolute relief, I hear the clank of the bell around her neck as she begins to follow me, bleating mournfully as she walks, as though to say, "Can you believe the morning I've had?" I almost bleat back.

"Good lord," I hear the boy murmur as other bells begin clanking. I risk a glance behind me to see, with a spurt of unexpected glee, that the other goats are falling into line.

"Do you have any more of those apples?" I call out to the old man, who procures another from a grubby bag that has spilled from the overturned cart and throws it to me. Catching it neatly in one hand, I nip around the side of the wooden crate, to the very far corner, and push the apple in through the slats. The nanny goat walks through the door, heading straight for the apple, and the other goats follow.

"And that," I say, pushing the door shut and fastening it with the brown ribbon that I pull from my hair, "is how you herd goats."

To his credit, the boy stands and applauds, those golden curls glinting in the sunlight. "Well done," he says, sincerely, as I push my hair envy away. "Though I do wish I'd thought to ask about apples a lot earlier."

I can't help but laugh. "If you think an apple would have helped you . . ."

The teeth flash, and a dimple appears. "Well, it couldn't have made things worse."

"Ahem." Lady Cassandra clears her throat conspicuously, and I jump, remembering where I am. I am glad she has been smart enough not to use my name, but I am kicking myself nonetheless for getting distracted by small talk. It isn't part of the plan at all.

"We must go," my lady continues.

"Oh, but can you help me turn this cart before you go?" The charming smile is back, the blue eyes upon me.

"If it's quick," I say, keeping my expression neutral, and adjusting my hood back around my face. He'd seen it, of course, and my hair when I'd whipped the ribbon out of it, but, as my mother has told me from birth, mine is not a memorable face. Not that it bothers me. Combined with mid-brown hair, blah brown eyes and enough common sense to stay silent when it suits me, my forgettable face serves me well.

Fortunately, the boy seems to take my lead — rather like a goat — for the small talk dries up as we push the cart upright. I look to the crate, now full of goats, still on the road.

"I'm afraid that your next problem will be getting the crate onto the cart," I say.

He looks nonplussed. "I hadn't thought of that," he says. "I don't suppose . . ."

"Maven!" Now my lady's voice is impatient, and I simply shake my head at the boy's beseeching eyes and cross back toward my waiting mare.

"May I help you remount?" he asks, following me across the road.

"I can get on my own horse," I respond, putting one foot in the stirrup and vaulting into the saddle. There had been a time when I'd envied the men and boys around me their breeches, but over the years I've pushed the boundaries of my limited life as far as practicable and have learned to do everything I need to do in a skirt. And if my skirts, made to my own design for the last few years, have always been too plain and too sensible to ever be in fashion, so be it. At least I will always have pockets, and will never have to ride sidesaddle like my sisters.

Fortunate, too, that, unlike my sisters, I have no need to mourn the life I once had. The plain dress of a servant suits me well.

"Come," says Lady Cassandra, whose voluminous traveling cloak hides the fact that her emerald-green dress is rucked up around her knees. She nudges her horse forward, and I follow, barely glancing at the crate of bleating goats and never looking back. She has mentioned my name, I realize, but my hope is that he will be so caught up with his goat crisis he will never remember.

"Will we still make it by nightfall?" Lady Cassandra asks, once we've ridden along the road, deeper into the forest, away from listening ears.

"As long as we don't spend too long with the Beech Circle," I respond.

"We'll spend as long as it takes," she retorts, before digging her heels into the horse's side and taking off at a gallop.

I urge my horse forward and follow, knowing that we are racing headlong into trouble.

CHAPTER TWO

"**A**re you ready?"

Reeve managed a tiny nod, not so much as glancing up as Lorimer, Steward of the Household, spoke. Reeve was pretty sure that the granite planes of Lorimer's face hadn't cracked a smile in decades.

"Don't forget what I told you," sniffed Lorimer, before raising his pale, veined hand to knock briskly on the polished wooden door, once, twice, thrice.

Time seemed to slow down for Reeve as each thump on the door resounded the length and breadth of the stone hallway. His mind raced through the last-minute instructions that Lorimer had fired off in the minutes since Reeve had clattered, late, into the great courtyard, almost falling off his horse in his haste.

Now, in the aching seconds between each knock, the memory of Lorimer's reedy voice went round and round in Reeve's mind. "Eyes down, don't speak unless spoken to, address Airl Buckthorn as 'your excellency,' Sir Garrick Sharp as 'sire,' approach only from the left, never the right . . ."

Reeve shook his head, trying to gather his scattered thoughts. He knew all of this. Hadn't Lady Rhoswen spent the last nine years teaching Reeve to know his laird from his lady? He'd done his time as a page – and then some.

"Enter," came a deep, rich voice from behind the door, and Reeve took a moment to wipe his clammy palms on his tight-fitting black hose. He'd been so proud to don them just a few short hours ago, for they, and the black tunic emblazoned with the bright-blue fox he wore, marked him, finally, as being in the service of Sir Garrick Sharp, Knight Protector of Rennart Castle, as surely as if he'd had the man's name tattooed on his forehead.

As the foremost knight in the fief of Rennart – and, it was said, the fiercest fighter and firmest hand when it came to law and order in the whole kingdom of Cartreff – Sir Garrick's fearsome reputation strode before him, and now Reeve would follow behind. Assuming that Sir Garrick and Airl Buckthorn forgave the fact that Reeve was late for their very first meeting . . .

Lorimer sniffed again. "Straighten that belt," he said, before turning the knob and sweeping through the door ahead of Reeve.

Adjusting his thick black leather belt so that the clasp sat right on his belly button and the sword nestled against his hip, Reeve raised his heels ever so slightly and walked lightly into the room behind Lorimer, making almost no sound. He kept his expression impassive, trying to smooth out any evidence of his nerves – and to bury his burning curiosity.

"Reeve of Norwood," Lorimer announced, his flat tone hiding the scorn he'd exhibited moments before.

"Ah, at last," said the deep voice as Reeve swept into a low bow. "We've been expecting you."

Lorimer sniffed again. "It seems, your excellency, that your new squire has problems with punctuality."

Reeve could feel a hot tide of embarrassment creeping up his face, but he kept his eyes down and said nothing. The Airl would care little about the recalcitrant goats that had made Reeve late – even less for a tale of how long it had taken Reeve to find two men to help him get the crate of said goats back onto a wagon.

"Now, now, Lorimer," said Airl Buckthorn. "The lad is used to the more relaxed ways of women at Harding Manor. Sir Garrick will soon have him dancing to a different tune."

Reeve swallowed his response, knowing that now was not the time or place to defend Lady Rhoswen and her household. Lady Rhoswen took her duties very seriously, and the Manor, and the farms around it that supplied the food for Rennart Castle, ran like clockwork. Given that the Airl was married to Lady Rhoswen, Reeve knew that he had spoken in jest — but Lorimer seemed mollified by the idea that his own stewardly skills were superior.

"Ah, my lord, there is no one I would rather have in charge of training of any nature than my Lady Rhoswen, as you well know." The laconic words came from a shadowy corner to Reeve's right. "She has done a superior job on her husband, after all."

So far, Reeve had managed to suppress his urge to stare around the solar and drink in the details, but his curiosity nearly won out — as it so often did — at this comment. Lady Rhoswen always spoke fondly of Sir Garrick but, even so, Reeve was taken aback at the level of familiarity the knight showed with the Airl.

Then again, why should Reeve be surprised? Was he himself not here as a wedding gift to that very knight? And, despite the fact that Reeve's father was Baron of Norwood, and Sir Garrick's title was one of honor, not birth, Reeve could not be happier with the arrangement.

Reeve knew from experience that titles counted for little in a fight. Being heir to his father's title had not protected Reeve's older brother, Larien, from the sharp blade of a broadsword. Now, Larien was sitting at home at Norwood Manor, an invalid for life – albeit one who would, as the oldest son, inherit their father's title, the manor and all the lands that went with it.

"Now, now," the Airl responded with an easy chuckle. "It is true the Lady Rhoswen is a fine judge of people and horses. It is why I took her recommendation on board for your new squire."

"Ah yes, the new squire," Sir Garrick said. "Look up, boy, so I can get the measure of you."

Reeve followed his instructions, squinting against the afternoon sunlight pouring in through the enormous window behind Airl Buckthorn's desk, trying his best to appear as tall and broad as he could. Reeve might be a gift to Sir Garrick, but that did not mean the man could not return him, unopened, so to speak, if he wished.

At sixteen, Reeve was well aware that this was his absolute last chance to train as a knight – with the honor, purpose and, most importantly, the separate income that entailed. If Sir Garrick rejected him, no one else would take him on, and Reeve might as well begin planning for banishment at eighteen. His father would not let him, as he put it, "loaf about Cartreff, leeching off his brother," and would dispatch him to sea on the first ship he could find "to make his own way in the world."

"Hmmm," said Sir Garrick, sounding as though he

was assessing horseflesh. "There's not much of him. And he's past the age most first become squires . . ."

Reeve stared straight ahead, his desire to display perfect courtly behavior warring within him with a ferocious urge to face Sir Garrick. The knight had never accompanied Airl Buckthorn on his rare visits to Harding Manor, being left behind to keep Rennart Castle ticking over in the Airl's absence. But Reeve had heard so much about the man in stories and songs that he'd built up a picture in his mind of what Sir Garrick looked like. And Reeve was currently picturing a dark-haired, broody man wearing an expression of displeasure.

Reeve's heart sank. That he needed to become a knight in order to stay in the kingdom of Cartreff was one thing. But he also desperately wanted to learn from the finest knight in the kingdom. Reeve's father had agreed to the squiring arrangement against his mother's objections that Sir Garrick was beneath the Norwood family socially, and Reeve was fairly certain his father had only agreed because he thought that Reeve would fail. In the baron's eyes, Reeve had never been as good as Larien at anything. And if Larien had taken a sword to the stomach, what hope did Reeve have of even making it through his training? One knight was as good as another because Reeve would never amount to much anyway.

"Tall enough, though," said Airl Buckthorn, breaking into Reeve's thoughts. "Whippy arms by the looks of him. Good-sized feet. He'll get bigger. Rhoswen held on to him for you."

"Hmmm," was the only response.

Reeve felt heat wash over his face, and he finally gave in to the impulse to slide his glance sideways. It didn't help much. If Airl Buckthorn was a solid silhouette against the stained glass windows, Sir Garrick presented as a patchwork of shadows.

"Rhoswen gave him glowing reports, so you can take it up with her when she arrives on the morrow," Airl Buckthorn continued, drawing Reeve's eyes back to him. "Given that at this stage the heaviest thing he'll have to carry is a plate, he'll do enough to earn his keep."

Plate? Reeve tried not to frown at the Airl's words.

"Indeed," agreed Sir Garrick. "And a good thing, methinks. The weight of a sword might just about do him in." There was a pause before the knight's voice came again. "I'm not sure about that hair, though."

Reeve blinked. What on earth could be wrong with his hair? Lady Rhoswen had always loved his blond ringlets. Even that odd peasant girl on the road had stared at them.

"Ye-e-es," said Airl Buckthorn. "It will have to go. Lorimer, see to it."

"As you wish, your excellency," said Lorimer, and Reeve winced at the relish in the man's voice. "Will that be all, your excellency? Sire?"

"Yes," said the Airl with a wave. "Get him settled.

Tomorrow morning will be soon enough to get him started. In the meantime, feed him up – let's get a little meat on those long bones. And Lorimer –"

The steward waited.

"Less of the 'your excellency,'" the Airl said with a grimace. "Airl is sufficient – and shorter."

Lorimer bowed, though Reeve could see his lips pucker as though he'd sucked down a lemon, and Reeve waited a moment before turning to follow the steward from the room at the correct distance. As he walked toward the door, Sir Garrick spoke again, in a voice just loud enough for Reeve to hear.

"Is he really the best you can do?"

"Cream of the crop, according to Rhoswen – and who are we to argue?" said Airl Buckthorn, not bothering to speak softly. "But let us talk of more important things. Tomorrow, the Fire Star will be here at Rennart Castle. In a few short days, you shall be wed. There is much to do."

"Indeed," Reeve heard Sir Garrick say as Reeve pulled the solid door behind him. He couldn't help but take note of the undertone of gloom in the brave knight's voice.

"'Ave another, young sire – those first six barely touched the sides."

Reeve wiped a trickle of syrup from his chin with the inside of his sleeve and patted his stomach. "No, really, Mistress Agnes, I couldn't fit in another morsel."

Indeed, the roiling sensation behind his belt suggested to Reeve that he should perhaps have foregone the sixth fig tart, but they had been so small and delicate – and delicious.

"Call me Cook," said Mistress Agnes, tapping him on the head with her ladle. "Perhaps you lost your stomach with your hair."

Looking up into her kind, lined face, Reeve couldn't help but blush.

Cook laughed, clutching her worn apron as though to contain her mirth. "Look!" she screeched. "Even the tips of his ears go red – and they're so easy to see now!"

Reeve blushed harder as the entire kitchen staff, right down to the pot boy, came to a standstill to stare.

"Leave him be," came a voice from the other side of the long wooden table, where Neale of Broadfield, Sir Garrick's other squire, concentrated on mopping up the syrup on his own plate with a skerrick of pastry. Reeve considered the dark, bent head opposite, surprised by the other boy's defense – particularly given he'd barely spoken a word to Reeve since Lorimer had left Reeve under Neale's supervision an hour before.

But Neale hadn't finished.

"He's suffering a great loss, you know ... Dead

attached he was to those curls."

As Cook roared with laughter, Reeve ran a rueful hand over the bristle on his scalp. Lorimer had taken Airl Buckthorn's directive to "see to" Reeve's hair very seriously, taking to his blond ringlets with a pair of shears. The meticulously symmetrical bob that Lady Rhoswen demanded all male members of her household sport was gone, leaving behind barely a finger's width of stubble all over. And it seemed as though the story of his haircut had spread like wildfire through the castle.

"Ah now, don't take on so," said Cook, patting Reeve's shoulder, the flour on her apron leaving a white mark on his tunic as it brushed against him. "Right manly you look now. Just right for a squire to our Sir Garrick. You and Neale are quite the pair — him so dark and you so fair. You'll make quite the splash in the wedding parade."

Neale popped the last bite of pastry into his mouth, his cheek working furiously as he chewed, appraising Reeve, his eyes cold.

"Perhaps," Neale conceded, looking up at Cook before reaching across the table with sticky fingers and pinching Reeve's cheek, hard. "But it hasn't helped his baby face. Or the fact that he's apparently a slow learner who needed two extra years as a page . . ."

Stung by both the pinch and the remark, Reeve stared into Neale's smirking face as the kitchen staff erupted into laughter around him. The other boy had made it clear from their first meeting that he didn't think that Sir Garrick needed a second squire, going so far as to suggest that Reeve should simply "go back home" to Lady Rhoswen.

But Reeve had been at Harding Manor since the age of seven, with no one to watch out for him amid the hurly-burly cut and thrust of daily life in a busy household. He had the feeling that Neale had taken one look at his blond ringlets and the face that Lady Rhoswen had always described as "pleasing," and had decided that Reeve was weak.

"It is difficult indeed to change one's face," Reeve said now, keeping his tone even as he brushed the dusting of flour from his shoulder. "Which is more of a penalty for some than others."

Neale's face darkened and twisted as the insult hit home, and Reeve stood up, allowing no hint of a smile to tilt his lips, even as the kitchen staff again erupted into howls of laughter. He would say no more at this time, particularly on the point of why he was a late-blooming squire, but he would stay on his toes around Neale, who was clearly protective of his position with Sir Garrick.

For the past two years, Neale had been the knight's only squire. Now, Neale would care for Sir Garrick's arms and armor as Battle Squire. He would also act as

Squire of the Body, assisting Sir Garrick in his chambers morning and evening.

But, as Airl Buckthorn had hinted in his comment about "plates," Reeve was to take over as Squire of the Table, serving Sir Garrick at meals, accompanying him in public duties.

It wasn't quite what Reeve had imagined when he'd spent hour after hour in the courtyard at Harding Manor practicing with his sword, working on his horse-riding skills atop a huge destrier or loosing arrow after arrow at the target set up on the green.

That was okay for now, for Reeve had learned many things over the course of nine years at the sleeve of Lady Rhoswen. On the surface, his daily lessons in her household had been about chivalry, courtesy, etiquette and valor, but he had also absorbed many skills from simply watching the lady manage her servants and move through society.

"The Carruthers are down on their luck," Lady Rhoswen would say, soaking her swollen feet after attending a pompous and expensive ball at the home of Lord and Lady Carruthers. "The artworks have been carefully rearranged to hide the gaps where they've sold off pieces – but you can never quite hide the darker wallpaper where they once hung."

Lies and deception were her favorite things to winkle out, and she delighted in sharing her findings with Reeve.

"Did you notice how she paused before answering every question?" Lady Rhoswen would ask when a kitchen maid had been discovered stealing precious honey. "Honest people don't do that."

On another occasion, a young stable boy had come undone during questioning about an injured horse. "His lips were saying no, but did you notice that almost imperceptible nod?" Lady Rhoswen asked Reeve later. "Our bodies are sometimes more honest than our minds."

Lady Rhoswen's daughter Anice hadn't understood her mother's interest in what Anice called "a lowly squire," but Lady Rhoswen had laughed. "It amuses me," she said. "Reeve is a good student, and you never know when such an eye for detail will come in handy."

One of the more useful tips she'd ever given Reeve, however, was to watch people's feet. "If I am talking to someone and I wish you to interrupt me with a message," she told him with a tinkling laugh, very early during his days at Harding Manor, "my feet will be pointed away from the person, to one side, almost as though I am ready to escape."

Right now, the anger in Neale's face told Reeve that it was time for his own feet to be leaving the kitchen. "Thank you kindly for the fine meal, mistress," he said to Cook. "But now I must prepare to assist Sir Garrick at table."

Cook's bushy eyebrows flew up. "I thought you weren't to start until the morrow," she said. "I could use an extra pair of hands here, what with the wedding feast to prepare and all."

"No time like the present," said Reeve, with a smile and a courtly bow, "and I'm sure Neale will be happy to assist, given Sir Garrick will not require him until much later."

Ducking out through the kitchen door before Neale could respond, Reeve considered the evening ahead. He'd decided to appear at table on his first night to prove to Sir Garrick that he was a worthy squire, an asset rather than the liability the knight seemed to believe he was.

As Reeve mounted the stairs that would take him to the labyrinth of long stone hallways that stretched to his room, which was tucked away in a corner of the west wing, he went over his plan. Reeve would change into a fresh tunic, one that was not wrinkled from the road and sprinkled with goat hair and the fine reminders of his haircut, and would be standing beside Sir Garrick's chair ten minutes before the evening feast was scheduled to begin.

Tonight was a special dinner indeed, he knew, for it was the last night that Sir Garrick would have at Rennart Castle before his bride-to-be arrived the following day.

It was an interesting time to be entering a new household, and Lady Rhoswen had told him to keep his wits about him.

"You will have not one new person to manage, but two, and my niece Cassandra can be . . . strong-willed," she had said to him with a sigh during their last, low-voiced conversation. "It is not the best time for you to begin, but Airl Buckthorn will not be dissuaded from this idea to give Sir Garrick a squire as a wedding present, and it was the opportunity I have long awaited for you."

Reeve grimaced now as he approached the solid wooden door of his room, slipping inside and bolting it behind him before letting out his breath with a whoosh as he flopped on the bed. His head throbbed, and Reeve wondered if it was exploding with all the new things he'd taken in since his arrival at Rennart Castle — or the tension he could feel buzzing within the walls.

He'd often felt like this after a day negotiating the various personalities and politics of Harding Manor, but Reeve had a very bad feeling that Rennart Castle would prove to be even more difficult. Indeed, hadn't Lady Rhoswen often said that one reason she preferred to stay at Harding Manor, a short distance away, was to avoid managing the "household wars" at Rennart?

Staring up at the swathes of deep-red velvet draping the top of his four-poster bed, Reeve realized that he needed to learn the ways of this castle quickly — or suffer the consequences.

Tonight would be his first test.

CHAPTER THREE

Standing behind Sir Garrick's chair at the top table, Reeve kept one eye on his master's pewter mug and one on the rowdy scene unfolding in front of him. Although the back of Sir Garrick's carved wooden seat was tall, Reeve was taller – a fact for which he was very thankful, since it allowed him to keep wary watch on the long table of house knights and minor lords on the right-hand side of the Great Hall, all of whom seemed determined to drain the castle's ale stores dry.

"Brantley is in his cups again," muttered Sir Garrick as he cleaned the last of the gravy from his trencher with a thick piece of bread.

"At least some are celebrating your last night as a free man, even if you are not," said Airl Buckthorn, leaning back in his own velvet-upholstered chair and grinning at Sir Garrick, who was now staring glumly into his own drink. "Good grief, man, you've barely touched your meal. Eat something or Cook will be wailing her offense into her stew pot."

Standing as still as a statue, Reeve nonetheless strained forward with every fiber to hear Sir Garrick's response. The man had seemed down in the mouth since arriving at the feasting table, which was groaning under the weight of a full roasted boar, whole baked fish, golden-crusted pies of fruit or game, round loaves of bread and three different wheels of cheese.

Reeve felt his belly rumble beneath his pristine tunic. The fig tarts were already feeling like a memory and it would be hours before he could follow them up with something more substantial. At least the noise in the hall was so deafening that no one was likely to hear his hunger pangs — not even Sir Garrick, the back of whose head was just inches from Reeve's stomach.

"It's not that I'm not grateful to my lord for the honor of marriage," Sir Garrick began.

"Not this again!" Airl Buckthorn groaned, waving away a servant who was trying to place a dish of stewed pears on the table before him. "You will not do better than this match, Garrick."

Reeve could see Sir Garrick's shoulders tighten under the fine linen tunic he wore. Reeve had no idea why the knight should be so tense about his own marriage, but his duty as a squire was to help the man if he could. Reeve stepped forward to offer Sir Garrick the thick napkin he had at the ready, knowing the knight would appreciate even the smallest amount of time to organize his thoughts.

Sir Garrick took it, pressing it carefully to his lips and thereby hiding his face for a moment. He handed the napkin back to Reeve, signaling his gratitude with the slightest lift of one eyebrow.

Reeve stepped back, suppressing a smile. He had done the right thing in choosing to present at the table that night. Sir Garrick had looked surprised to see him but had said nothing, and Reeve had gone about his duties as seamlessly as he knew how.

"It is not a question of the brilliance of the match, your excellency," Sir Garrick said now to Airl Buckthorn. "More a question of one's readiness for marriage."

Reeve's ears pricked up once again. Lady Rhoswen had hinted darkly several times that Sir Garrick's forthcoming nuptials were less about Sir Garrick's future happiness and more about the Airl's aspirations, but had never explained why.

"She is a noted beauty," said Airl Buckthorn, gulping down a large mouthful of ale. "My brother-in-law had many offers for her, even as the youngest of my four nieces, even as his fortune dwindled."

"Indeed," said Sir Garrick. "So many that he accepted the poor, dear, departed Sir Alfred Dumfries."

"Not so long departed," Airl Buckthorn quibbled.

"Not long after acceptance," Sir Garrick shot back.

There was a pause. "What's your point?" barked Airl Buckthorn, his face red.

Sir Garrick turned back to his pewter mug, taking a long swallow. "You know she wouldn't have accepted me if she wasn't desperate."

Airl Buckthorn's expression cleared and he clapped the knight on the back with a hearty guffaw. "She didn't accept you, fool," he said. "Her father accepted *me*, and very grateful he was, too. Cassandra has been left too much to her own devices since her mother – my only sister, I remind you – was taken by consumption ten years ago."

"I remain sorry for your loss – and hers," said Sir Garrick after a pause. "But the fact is that the castle is rife with scuttlebutt that Cassandra believes she is marrying down – she of noble birth, me of conferred honor."

Reeve had to cough to hide his sharp intake of breath. He had heard the rumors, even at Harding Manor, but had thought such talk confined to areas far from Sir Garrick's ears.

"Well, she is," said Airl Buckthorn, matter-of-factly, and now he gestured to the servant bearing the stewed pears, who placed them before the Airl. "And, given she is past twenty-five years of age and her former betrothed did not make it to the altar, my beloved niece Cassandra should be happy not to be collecting dust on a shelf for the rest of her natural life. What of it?"

A loud burst of laughter from the lower table drowned out Sir Garrick's next words, but did nothing to hide Airl Buckthorn's reaction.

"Is that all?" he hooted, looking up from his pears. "Dear lord, man, don't you knights spend years learning about chivalry and the like? Woo her, for God's sake. Win her over."

He turned to Reeve, who was struggling to hide his interest in the conversation.

"This young fellow will help you," Airl Buckthorn continued. "Won't you, Rove?"

"Er, it's Reeve," Reeve stammered, and not for the first time in his life. Despite regular visits to see his wife at Harding Manor, the Airl had never bothered to remember the name of her lowly squire. "And I will be honored. As Sir Garrick's squire I am bound to help him in all things."

Sir Garrick stared at him, his shrewd, almost-black eyes seeming to look right into Reeve's mind. "I believe that you believe that," he said, before turning back to the

Airl. "All I can say is that I hope this Fire Star is worth it."

Reeve stared straight ahead over the two men's bent heads as they continued to talk in low voices. What was a Fire Star, he wondered, and why did Airl Buckthorn want it so much he'd marry his own niece off to his prize knight to get it?

Knights rarely married and, when they did, they didn't marry the daughters of barons, which Lady Cassandra most certainly was. Daughter of a baron, niece of an airl, she would, even as daughter number four, have been a catch for someone.

"You blaggard!"

The harsh cry split the air, followed by the grating slither of a sword being unsheathed. Reeve stood on his tiptoes, peering between Airl Buckthorn and Sir Garrick, who had both jumped to their feet at the sound — as had most of the hall.

The rowdy lower table had gone deathly quiet as an unkempt man in the Airl's colors waved a sword above his head, its sharp, polished blade catching the glow of the torches that lit the room.

"You take that back!" the man shouted, his unshaven face red with anger. "Take it back or I shall call you out."

"Ha!" retorted a chubby bald man, licking his sausage-like fingers with apparent disregard for the violent threats. "I'll not take back the truth, Brantley of Adelard. You will never be a knight, and you know it."

31

As Brantley bellowed an oath and began to swing the sword back to strike, Sir Garrick drew up to his full height and roared across the hall: "*Stop* in the name of the Airl of Buckthorn."

Brantley froze, his face paling beneath his stubble.

"You forget yourself," Sir Garrick continued in a deceptively mild voice, the undertone of menace so cold that Reeve stared at his new master in shock. "All weapons are checked at the door to this hall. Or did you forget?"

"I – er," Brantley stammered, sheathing his sword with a practiced movement. "I meant no harm, sire."

"I doubt that Derric there would agree," said Sir Garrick, stepping around the table and swaggering to the center of the hall. "Another moment and the back of his neck would have felt your lack of harm."

Brantley flushed a deeper red and said nothing.

"You may leave now," Sir Garrick said, with a smile that contained not a hint of amusement or friendliness. "All of you."

The men stood as one and filed out of the hall obediently, although Reeve noted that Brantley took his time, sauntering at the back of the line, and thought he even saw the man wink as he passed a table of young women. Given that the Lady Anice, Airl Buckthorn's own daughter, sat at the head of that table, however, Reeve thought he must have been mistaken – surely Brantley would not be so bold?

The Airl certainly did not seem to have seen a wink, and Lady Anice moved not one copper hair, even as her friends giggled and whispered. Either Reeve had imagined the wink, or Lady Anice had indeed developed the "social poise" she had convinced her father she would learn at Rennart Castle.

Until just a few years ago, Lady Anice had been resident at Harding Manor, where her difficult ways had made her unpopular with the servants. Reeve had learned from his earliest days as a page to stay away from the pretty girl with the ugly temper.

Reeve had heard that Lady Rhoswen had argued against Anice's move to Rennart Castle, knowing it would give Anice more freedom. The Airl believed his daughter could do no wrong – which meant that Anice could do pretty much anything.

But Anice had won – as she so often did – and maybe, Reeve thought now, Lady Rhoswen had been wrong.

"Thank you all for joining us tonight," Sir Garrick said, once all of the rowdy men had left the silent hall. His small bow managed to take in every man, woman and child at the crowded tables. "I am sure you all look forward to greeting the Lady Cassandra on the morrow, as much as I do. But now –"

"Oh, but why wait?" trilled a high, gleeful voice from the doorway, and Reeve stared in astonishment at the vision in bright green now entering the hall. "Why not greet me now?"

Sir Garrick's jaw dropped, but no voice came out and it was up to Airl Buckthorn to rise from the table and step smoothly forward.

"But what is this?" he asked in a jovial tone, though Reeve did not miss the irritation beneath the Airl's words. "My Lady Cassandra? We were not expecting you until mid-morning tomorrow."

"Ah, Uncle," Cassandra breathed, sweeping toward him in a swirl of skirts before dropping into a deep and elegant curtsey. "How could I wait a moment longer to meet the man you have decreed I marry?"

CHAPTER FOUR

As the last of the banished men have shuffled off down the hallway, I creep out of the shadows and peer around the door like a child to watch what is happening in the Great Hall. Cassandra is playing it like the finest mummer, and the people assembled at the tables can do nothing but stare, open-mouthed, at the performance. Inwardly, I am applauding, though I stay as quiet as a mouse.

Objectively, I can see that my lady was right to insist on wearing the emerald-green gown. She is beautiful, with her dark brows winging over the wide-set eyes that match her dress perfectly. The fine white lace outlining the deep square neckline of the richly embroidered bodice sets it off perfectly. It. The huge, sparkling red stone that rests in the hollow of her throat, secured by a thin, black, velvet ribbon. The reason we are all here.

The Fire Star. A jewel worth a king's ransom.

The room seems to pause at the sight of it, a deep silence before the whispers begin. I have seen hen's eggs smaller than the stone, which seems to burn from within like the red-hot embers of a dying fire.

It's a dazzling display of wealth — and a family secret revealed.

I know not the name of the woman who first wore this jewel, nor how it came to be in Cassandra's family. All I know is what Cassandra has told me, and she knows little enough herself.

The Fire Star has been passed down from youngest daughter to youngest daughter, across the generations, bequeathed only on the occasion of that youngest daughter's betrothal. It cannot be used as a dowry, nor even mentioned to a potential suitor before that day.

When I asked Cassandra how it was possible, in this day and age in Cartreff, that such a valuable stone remain within the hands of women for so long, she laughed without mirth.

"Sorcery," she'd said, "or rumors thereof. Grandmother told me that the story goes that the Fire

Star is cursed and 'pitiless bad luck' befalls any man who tries to take ownership. It must remain in the hands of women."

"Sorcery? Pitiless bad luck?" I responded.

Cassandra had managed another laugh. "Sorcery is the word applied to anything that women do that men do not understand, and the Fire Star is no different. It is held by the youngest daughter, safe for the next generation, and never talked about. Apparently, the women in my family have done much to keep the story alive and absolutely nothing to clarify any details at any time . . . and so the myth of the Fire Star has grown."

Unfortunately, the myth had been exposed beyond the reach of immediate family when dear old Sir Alfred had been convinced by Cassandra's father to marry Cassandra, and then died before reaching the altar.

But not before he'd shared news of his good fortune with several of his friends, and word had reached Airl Buckthorn.

"I don't understand why the Airl didn't organize this marriage much sooner." I had been packing her trunks for the journey to Rennart Castle when I'd mused those words aloud, and she had snorted like a horse at my innocence.

"He did not know about the Fire Star until Sir Alfred's death," she'd said.

"But surely your mother, his sister, mentioned it?" I had been focused on placing bags of lavender among the garments folded into the trunk, but did not miss the small silence that followed my words.

"She did not know," Cassandra said, her voice flat. "My father is an only child, a boy, and the stone remained with my grandmother Jeanne until her death, willed to me, the youngest daughter, in a sealed codicil that remained unread until the day of my betrothal."

Once he knew the stone was there for the taking, Airl Buckthorn had pounced, offering Sir Garrick as a consolation prize to the "bereft" bride – Sir Garrick who is bound to the Airl by an oath of loyalty until death.

"Isn't the Airl afraid of sorcery and 'pitiless bad luck'?" I'd asked Cassandra when she'd told me the plan.

"The secret of the Fire Star is out, and the Airl wants it under his roof and his control," Cassandra had answered. "Once I am married, my father demands that I give the stone to my cousin Anice as a 'gratitude gift' for being saved by her family from spinsterhood. My husband, who takes ownership of me upon marriage, will not object. And so the Fire Star will go, woman to woman, into the Buckthorn family tree."

Even now, as I watch the outwardly polite battle of wills being fought by the Airl and Cassandra, I have to admit that the plan is neat. The stone will technically remain in the hands of a woman – Anice – neatly sidestepping the "pitiless bad luck." But, as his daughter, Anice and all her possessions belong to the Airl, bringing him ownership of the Fire Star in all but name.

The same Airl, resplendent in a tunic embroidered all about with silver thread, is clearing his throat in the Great Hall. He towers over my Lady Cassandra, and, despite being at least forty-five years of age, remains lean. Lady Cassandra does nothing but wait, her hands on her skirts, allowing him – and everyone else in the Great Hall – to understand what it is that she brings to this castle in the boondocks of Cartreff. To this knight, who is so far beneath her in status.

To the casual observer, her pose is demure, even deferential, to her uncle, but the message is clear. I, who know her well, can see the set of her jaw, the glitter in those lovely eyes. I suppress a smile, knowing what it is costing her not to attack her uncle and rake her nails across his face.

But she won't do this. I know it. She knows it. So does the Airl.

"You forget yourself, my lady," he says, mildly enough, but she stiffens. "We are not ready for you and your party."

Cassandra laughs, and I wince at the shriek barely hidden by the dramatic giggle, but she tosses back her head in such a way as to set the stone dancing once more, its sparkle seeming to reach even the darkest corners of the hall.

"There is no party, Uncle," Cassandra says, her tone measured. "I came on ahead. The rest will follow tomorrow, as expected."

The Airl freezes. "You are unescorted?" he says, unable to hide his surprise or displeasure. "At night? In these dangerous times?"

"Not unescorted," Cassandra retorts, swinging her dark plait over her shoulder, where it slithers down her back. "Maven has many talents."

I smirk, pressing as close to the wall beside the open door as I dare. It will not do to be discovered lurking out here.

"Maven?" says a man behind him. The blue fox on his tunic gives him away, and I study him with interest. This is the man my lady is expected to marry. Dark-haired, heavy lidded, strong. Many would think that she could do worse, I know. But not my Lady Cassandra.

As the youngest of four daughters, she has always felt her expendability. And so it has always been her dearest wish to prove them wrong. To marry well. To marry better than any of them and have the pleasure of making them, the other three, bow and scrape in her presence as they have made her do to them these many long years.

For that, she needs a duke at least, and, oh, she had come so close. But that dream had died with Sir Alfred, and so, here we are.

Marrying Sir Garrick will consign her to the very bottom of the pecking order forevermore. And it is for this reason that it will never, ever happen. Not if my Lady Cassandra has anything to do with it.

"My companion," Lady Cassandra is saying, ostentatiously not turning so much as a hair to look at her outraged uncle. "Enough of an entourage for *this* occasion."

It is all I can do not to laugh as I watch Sir Garrick stiffen, absorbing the snub almost as though Cassandra has hit him. His squire hands him a napkin, and Garrick busies himself wiping nonexistent crumbs from his mouth, hiding his response from the crowded hall. It's a nice move by anyone's standards, and I crane forward to catch a glimpse of the exemplary, quick-thinking servant, who is shrinking back as I recognize this morning's goat herder – minus the curls, which appear to have been shorn.

Interesting. Perhaps there is more to that pretty face than I'd first thought.

"Very well," Airl Buckthorn says, drawing my gaze back to him. He turns toward the crowd – still seated at their tables, most not even trying to hide their interest in the drama playing out – and claps his hands.

"It seems that we are blessed with the presence of the bride a night earlier than expected!" the Airl says, before pausing. A few people in the closest seats try a feeble cheer, which quickly dies away. I wish I could see the Lady Cassandra's face right now, but it's probably for the best. One glance at me and we are both likely to descend into a gale of laughter.

"Indeed," the Airl continues, "it is a joyous occasion, but she is tired and will retire to her rooms now as we enjoy dessert."

Many might miss the subtle nod the Airl sends in the direction of the jongleur in the corner, but I do not. As the man raises his lute and begins picking out a lively air, I drift inside the hall, creeping along the wall while everyone's attention is on the musician. Moments later, servants burst through the doors with tray upon tray of wobbly jelly, golden tarts filled with creamy custard, and pears glistening with red-wine syrup. Before long, the crowd is oohing and aahing over the sweet treats, talking among themselves at an ever-rising volume.

Lady Cassandra, however, does not move, and I creep closer, just near enough to catch her next words. "I see you are not pleased to see me, Uncle," she hisses beneath the music.

Airl Buckthorn smiles as though she's made a jest, before speaking in a tone so low that only those in the immediate vicinity could possibly hear.

"You have had the entrance you wished for," he says. "You are lucky that's all you've had. You took a great risk riding here alone tonight – the roads are not safe now, particularly for a woman like you."

My ears prick up at his words. Beyond the gossip about the King, we have heard the other rumors of unrest. Of the sovereign's favorites who are picked up one minute and then discarded the next, stripped of titles and lands which are then handed to others like sweets. Of those who believe the King should be encouraged to marry and produce an heir – so that he can be replaced. Of peasants, tired of working only to pay taxes, who walk off the land to roam the roads, stealing what they can from passing travelers. But no men ever speak to women about politics, so thirdhand stories are all we have.

"I haven't the slightest idea what you mean," says Lady Cassandra, staring him down. "We saw nothing untoward beyond some King's horsemen and a farmer who'd lost control of his goats. And I assume it is not my safety you are concerned for, but that which I bring to you as a wedding gift."

"King's horsemen, you say? Then you were lucky," says the Airl, ignoring her last words, and for one heart-stopping moment I think he will forget himself and say more. "But we will not speak of it now. You may retire to your rooms – I am sure you need a good night's rest."

"Oh no," says Cassandra, gaily, moving as though to step around him and take a seat at the table. "I fancy some black currant jelly."

Once again, I nearly break into applause. In the candlelight, her cheeks flushed, she is so beautiful and so dangerous. She will win the hearts of these people simply by sitting there among them. Which, of course, her uncle also realizes.

"My lady, you do not," the Airl replies, and this time the tone of his voice stops her in her tracks, the green gown swirling around her boots. Boots, I note now as the Airl and Cassandra glare at each other, that are still dusty from the road. I sigh. No doubt others will notice this and it will be me, the maid, who bears the brunt, not Cassandra the Impatient.

"Very well," Cassandra finally sniffs, "you may have some choice morsels sent to my rooms."

And she now flings that long rope of hair back over her shoulder and draws herself up to her full height before stalking toward Sir Garrick, who takes an almost indiscernible step back. I also shrink back along the wall. With my brown dress, brown hair and skin tanned by what Mother has always called "an unseemly attraction to the outdoors," I know that I blend in to the stone backdrop, allowing me a few more moments to observe.

"And you must be my betrothed," Cassandra says, her voice shrill with a mixture of frustration and anger. "You may kiss my hand."

She sticks her fingers under his nose, radiating

defiance. Taken aback, Sir Garrick hesitates, and it's as though the room holds its breath, awaiting his next move. Knights are trained to be chivalrous and courteous at all times. Surely, the greatest knight in the kingdom won't fail now, with his very own betrothed?

But no. Sir Garrick's face relaxes into a gentle smile, and he takes her fingers in his own and leans forward to graze the top of her hand. Transfixed, it takes me a moment to remember we hate him.

"Enchanted," he murmurs, and even I hear my lady's indrawn breath. Or perhaps it is my own.

But she gives no outward sign of appeasement, instead snatching the hand back a moment before it is courteous and whirling about to sketch a cursory curtsey in her uncle's direction. I scuttle back to my position in the hallway by the door.

"I look forward to a lengthy discussion on the morrow," I hear the Airl say as Cassandra strides toward the door. She gives no sign of having heard the dark tone of his words, no sign beyond pulling the door behind her shut with more force than was necessary.

I grip her arm, my finger on my lips to silence any outburst, and march her at pace down the hallway. As we walk, I can hear the hubbub of conversation begin again, with bursts of raucous laughter amidst the discussion.

A footman materializes out of the darkness by the magnificent stone staircase that leads up and away to the accommodation wings of the castle.

"Just tell us how to get to my lady's quarters and leave us," I snap. Cassandra is melting beside me as he gives directions, her energy sapped by our long day and the courage required for the performance she has just managed.

As I struggle up the stairs with her, the footman watching us all the way, I whisper, "Not long, my lady. Stay strong. Appearances are everything."

Cassandra takes heed, straightening up, recognizing, as I do, that every move we make in this place will be reported upon, dissected, discussed.

"How did I do?" she asks me, and I can hear in her voice her need for affirmation. That Cassandra gets it only from her fifteen-year-old maid sums up most of what has brought her – and me – to this place.

"Fine," I say. "But let us not speak of it until we reach our quarters."

"The wheels are in motion," Cassandra says, her free hand creeping up to clutch the stone at her throat, where it continues to sparkle even in the dim light of the hall.

"They are." I nod, finally reaching our door and pushing it open. "But they have a long and bumpy road to travel before we reach our destination."

Later, as I place the Fire Star in a leather pouch

and tuck it inside my lady's jewel case, I think upon her words. I understand what drives her to the desperate action she has undertaken, and I will do everything in my power to help her. For if she succeeds, then so do I.

But that does not mean that I am confident.

Cassandra does not know the world as I do. Despite her despised position within her own family, she does not really understand that her family has a superior position within the world. Nor can she see the many, many souls who are worse off. Souls who would tear her family down in an instant if it meant bettering their own lot even a tiny bit.

But I see it. I know. I have been there. I may be ten years younger than my lady, but the truth is that I am worlds older than she.

And so, after I have unbraided her hair and brushed the glossy strands until they gleam, after I have washed her feet in lavender-scented water, after I have tucked her beneath crisp linen sheets and drawn the velvet curtains — all while she talks and talks and talks of her plans, her dreams, her demons — only then do I slide from the dark room, closing the door behind me with the tiniest of clicks.

It is time for me to introduce myself to those members of the Beech Circle who dwell within the walls of Rennart Castle.

Our meeting at the Beech Circle sanctuary earlier

today was fruitful, and we have been offered all assistance — as we would give to others under different circumstances. It is a small chapter, but well resourced, with a leader who engenders trust, and members from all societal strata. I hope that we will have no need of the two members who reside at Rennart Castle, for I do not wish to deliver our troubles on others . . . but I am grateful to know they are nearby.

If all goes well, they will have received the message to meet and I will be back here within the hour.

If I am discovered — if the Beech Circle is discovered — I will not be back at all.

CHAPTER FIVE

As Reeve pulled back Sir Garrick's chair for his master to settle himself before the dessert selection, the knight turned to Airl Buckthorn.

"That went well," he remarked, trying for a light tone.

"She always was headstrong, that girl," Airl Buckthorn responded, his tone fierce.

Sir Garrick winced. "You never mentioned that when you were telling me how beautiful she was and how beneficial this marriage would be."

The Airl paused and then grinned. "My father once told me that Rhoswen was too headstrong to be a lady," he said, before slurping up a delicate mouthful of jelly.

"And?" Sir Garrick prodded after a moment.

"I don't think I need to add anything more," the Airl said.

"Too scared to add anything more, more like," Sir Garrick murmured under his breath before turning to his own dessert.

Reeve suppressed a smile even as he stood to attention behind the knight's chair. The idea of anyone daring to describe Lady Rhoswen as headstrong to her face was, indeed, laughable. But neither could he imagine the dignified older woman causing a scene like the one Lady Cassandra had made here tonight.

Reeve could already imagine the whispers of scandal leaking out from under the castle doors and into the wider world, where they would be pored over and dissected in parlors across the kingdom.

For Lady Cassandra to turn up unannounced the night before she was due was a big enough social crime. But for her to have come on her own, escorted only by a maid, and to boldly walk in here wearing that valuable stone without so much as doing her hair or wiping the dust from her boots . . .

The maid should have known better. Maven, Cassandra had called her, and Reeve had known immediately that these were the two he'd met on the road that afternoon. Cassandra had kept her head down, but the other . . .

Where had they been all these long hours since they'd left him? Reeve was still frowning over the question when the Airl spoke again.

"On the subject of headstrong, have we news of our friend?" he asked Sir Garrick.

Sir Garrick took an inordinate amount of time chewing his jelly before responding. "The only news is that there is no news," he said, looking glum. "Our pleas and the pleas of others who worry fall on deaf ears. He continues to spend Cartreff's coffers for his own ends, claiming that it is his birthright."

Airl Buckthorn sighed. "I was afraid of that," he said. "And, in the meantime, the dissent from the Great Families of the western fiefs grows louder, and I see factions rallying. They will not stand by as the kingdom goes broke, to be picked over by our enemies."

"Some in the North report they already hear whispers from beyond our borders," Sir Garrick revealed.

The Airl sat back in his chair, staring out over the Great Hall, where people were happily squabbling over the last skerricks of dessert and beginning to sit back in their own seats.

"Twenty-seven years of peace we enjoyed under his father, and he has managed to undo all of that in the space of just two years," Airl Buckthorn said. "You won't remember the last war, but I do, and the soil of Cartreff ran with blood – our own blood. It must be avoided at all costs."

Sir Garrick was now also staring straight ahead, as though the two men were not really speaking to each other at all. "You know what it is that you say," he said. "Dangerous words for dangerous times."

"I do," said the Airl, turning to look the Knight Protector square in the face. "I do. God knows I wish that they were words that could be unsaid, but I fear that these and worse will be uttered over and over before the year is out. Cartreff will not survive his reign."

"You will be labeled a traitor for even speaking of such things," said Sir Garrick, "and you have heard the rumors of spies, as I have . . ." Reeve felt the hairs on the back of his neck stand up as he realized at last what the two men were discussing. He glanced around, seeing no one within earshot except Neale, who was ambling past without even acknowledging Reeve's presence.

"This I know," the Airl said with a heavy sigh, as Reeve focused once more on the conversation. "But to do nothing would be to stand as a bigger traitor to this kingdom. I cannot stand by and watch as all that is good and fair about Cartreff is put to the sword by a king who cares only for himself and his pleasure. King Bren must be convinced to change . . . or the king must be changed."

Sir Garrick nodded. "I am your man, as always. What you need done, I will do."

"Excellent," said Airl Buckthorn, looking relieved.

"The first thing you can do is to get married. It will secure the alliance with my brother-in-law and —"

He broke away with a smile.

"And?" Sir Garrick asked.

"There is no better cover for a war counsel than a wedding," said Airl Buckthorn. "By the time you have a wife, our plans will be underway."

"Hmmm," said Sir Garrick, as Reeve refilled his mug with ale. "And I will be off to war. This could be the shortest marriage in the history of marriages."

Airl Buckthorn laughed. "Given how pleased Cassandra was to see you this evening, that might not be a bad thing."

"Alas, your excellency," said Sir Garrick, taking a deep swallow from his mug, "I think you may be right."

CHAPTER SIX

Thursday

Rubbing bleary eyes, Reeve stumbled into the kitchen, nearly falling over a tiny scullery maid who carried a cooking pot half her size.

"Oi!" she said, in a surprisingly big voice. "Watch it, you oaf!"

"Sorry," Reeve mumbled as she darted off toward the huge hearth, where various pots and pans were steaming and sizzling.

"Come to give us that hand now, have you?" said Cook, stirring a cauldron of something that smelled like onions and beef broth. "We could use one."

"Er, no," said Reeve. "I'm to report to Lorimer straight

after breakfast." He rubbed the stubble on his head ruefully and smoothed his tunic, trying to look as though he was ready for duty. He suspected it was a big stretch. When the page had appeared at sunup with Lorimer's message, Reeve had been in bed not more than an hour.

"Where's Neale then?" Cook asked, sounding grumpy. "He'll do in a pinch."

"I don't know," Reeve said. "I haven't seen him."

His long night in the Great Hall had become even longer when, after eventually escorting Sir Garrick from the table as the last candles guttered and then half carrying the knight to his chambers, Reeve had discovered that Neale was absent. Instead, the room looked as though no one had been there for hours, the fire having burned down to coals and the thick quilt still drawn tightly up to the end of the bed.

Hadn't Reeve seen Neale leave the Great Hall during dessert? Surely he'd had ample time to prepare Sir Garrick's chamber? Either way, no matter how late the hour, Neale should have been waiting to assist Sir Garrick in his nightly routine.

Surprised and frowning, Reeve had wrangled Sir Garrick to the foot of the bed, wrestled his boots off and then dragged the by then gently snoring knight under the covers, drawing the velvet canopy around the bed against the morning sunlight, which was just a few short hours away.

Finally, Reeve had been able to steal away down the dark, silent hallway to his own quarters, still wondering where Neale could be. When a door had closed somewhere behind Reeve, the click echoing through the halls like a woodcutter's axe, he'd stopped dead, feeling the blood rush to his ears, wondering at his own jumpiness . . .

"Hummmph," said Cook, dropping a heavy lid on the pot with a clang that brought Reeve back to the present. "Typical Neale. Always skulking about somewhere else when there's work to be done. Not that you can say anything, given the temper on that lad. Goes off like a blacksmith's spark at the slightest bit of criticism."

Thinking of the thunderous expression on Neale's face during their exchange yesterday, Reeve nodded. He was not looking forward to having to discuss last night's lapse of duty with Neale, but also knew that if he let it pass this time, he'd be working night and day to cover for Neale for the rest of his life.

"And did you say breakfast?" Cook continued now, bringing him out of his dark thoughts. "You'd be lucky. Didn't you hear? The Lady Cassandra has arrived."

"And don't we all know it," muttered a flaxen-haired kitchen maid who was seated at the table, slicing carrots into thin sticks. A great pile of honey cakes sat cooling on a wire rack beside her, making Reeve's mouth water as their sweet scent wafted toward him.

Cassandra. Just her name conjured up that vision in green, the great red stone flashing at her throat. And the peasant girl in brown — Maven — whom Reeve had seen with her the day before. He wondered again just what it was that the pair of them had been doing for all of those hours between the goat incident and Cassandra's dramatic entrance in the Great Hall.

He frowned and reached for a honey cake, only to feel a sharp pain across his knuckles. "Do that again and I'll leave a bruise," warned Cook, brandishing the heavy metal spoon with which she'd slapped him.

Speaking of bruises, Reeve thought, as he flashed her a rueful smile, he could feel a big one blossoming across his ribs. Another factor in his sleepless night.

He'd waited a few moments after hearing the door shut and, when all was again silent, had begun creeping down the hallway, arriving in a large antechamber where three or four passageways connected. The torches in the room were flickering, almost at the end of their life, and shadows moved across the walls.

At least he'd thought they were shadows. Right up until a solid mass had hit him in the stomach, driving all of the breath from his body and sending him to his knees with a loud "oof."

Gasping, Reeve had heard running feet and realized that someone had barreled into him in the gloom. Whether he'd been felled by a punch or simply the glancing blow of contact with the headlong runner, he wasn't sure — but Reeve noticed that whoever it was didn't so much as hesitate in their flight to check he was okay.

Eyes watering, Reeve had risen slowly to his feet, gulping in air as he'd staggered back to his room, where he'd lain awake, tossing and turning as he pondered his long and troubling day.

"Oh wait, you were there," said Cook. She handed her spoon to the tiny scullery maid who stood up, moved to the stove and removed the huge pot lid with ease before standing on tiptoe to take up the rhythmic stirring while Cook advanced toward Reeve.

Reeve said nothing. Lady Rhoswen had always taught him that the best way to learn anything was to keep your mouth closed. And he'd learned very quickly that household politics shifted on a breeze and it never did to let anyone know where you stood on any matter. One memorable thrashing at the hands of the head groom — who'd overheard when Reeve had innocently agreed with another page that the Harding Manor horses were not the best he'd ever seen — had taught Reeve that lesson.

"Was it as bad as they say?" Cook asked, and Reeve took a step back at the avid curiosity in her eyes. "Was she disheveled? Is it true she traveled with *only* a maid?"

Reeve hesitated, thoughts whirling. The kitchen was not only the stomach of any household, but its very heart when it came to keeping abreast of important information. Reeve knew that anything he said now would be flying down the castle hallways within moments — and also that if he said nothing, he'd be ostracized forevermore.

For a moment, Reeve fancied he felt a jester's tightrope swaying beneath his feet.

"My Lady Cassandra did indeed arrive ahead of time last night," he said, slowly. "So keen was she to meet her betrothed."

Cook smirked.

"I heard that the Airl was not so *keen* to see her," she needled.

Reeve smiled easily in return, careful not to react. "Airl Buckthorn is always pleased to see family," he said. "As the Lady Rhoswen will be when she arrives today."

Cook nodded, acknowledging his artful changing of the subject.

"You will be pleased to see my lady," she said.

"Indeed."

"But not as pleased as Airl Buckthorn, I'd say," Cook continued, laughing raucously and turning on her heel to take the spoon back from the scullery maid. "A woman's touch will be required to bring Lady Cassandra to heel — and Lady Rhoswen is just the one to do it. I wish we saw more of her here at Rennart, but she knows her own mind, that one."

Reeve couldn't help but agree with Cook's summation, but he took care to show nothing of his thoughts. "The wedding will be a great day for all, and my Lady Rhoswen looks forward to it," was all he said.

Cook chuckled again before frowning. "Yes, well, it won't be a great day if I don't get some more help," she declared, and Reeve sighed inwardly – his mention of the wedding had deflected her interest, as he'd intended.

"Then I will get out of your way, mistress," he said, edging toward the door as Cook turned to berate the unfortunate scullery maid for not stirring the stew fast enough. As Reeve sidled past the table, he slipped a warm honey cake into the deep pocket of his tunic. He would have just enough time to wolf it down before he got to Lorimer's parlor.

Scurrying out through the kitchen door, Reeve turned left toward Lorimer's parlor under the stairs, before retrieving the honey cake and taking a big bite. He hoped that whatever the steward wanted wouldn't take too long. It wouldn't do to be late to table for Sir Garrick – though Reeve did wonder if the knight would make it to breakfast that morning.

"Better watch out. You wouldn't want to be caught stealing."

I keep a straight face as he whirls around at my words, nearly choking on the honey cake I watched him purloin as he left the kitchen.

He swallows hard, recovering his dignity with his breath as he realizes it is just me, a lowly servant girl, lounging against the wall. No one to cause him any trouble.

"We meet again," he says, and that annoying dimple appears briefly.

"Indeed," I respond. "You seem less . . . flustered this morning."

I can see him relax as he takes another bite of the honey cake, the scent of which wafts toward me, making my mouth water.

"Cat got your tongue?" I ask as he continues to chew thoughtfully. "Or are goat herding and thieving your only, er, skills?"

"No," he sputters, before pulling himself together. "I am but struck dumb by your loveliness."

I cannot contain a sharp crack of laughter. "Seriously? That's your response? And I thought you squires were supposed to be clever."

I watch, fascinated, as the tide of red rises over his cheeks. "You mock me, my lady?"

"Oh, put a stocking in it," I say. "Save your knightly speeches for a lady who will flutter her fan and her eyelashes at your charm."

The truth is, the whole notion of chivalry bores me. What is the point of taking part in a charade when there are real conversations to be had? Unfortunately, I am a rebellion of one when it comes to this radical idea. I have in turn appalled or offended boys, girls, men and women by trying to transform meaningless banter into something interesting.

Or so my mother likes to tell me. When she writes. Which is not often now.

But this boy is not turning away in disgust at my uncouth forwardness. Rather, he is studying me, apparently deep in thought. With a frown, it is true, but without the moue of disgust that often accompanies such close inspection of my forgettable face and "untoward mouth" (thank you, Mother).

Perhaps he is not averse to the notion of not having to be thinking one step ahead of every conversation and peppering it with ridiculously lavish compliments and other drivel? There must be at least one boy in the kingdom who agrees with me?

"As you wish," he says, finally, before popping the last of the honey cake into his mouth, his expression giving nothing more away. "We were not introduced yesterday, but I believe your name is Maven?"

"Yes, I'm Maven." I push myself upright and stroll toward him. "The Lady Cassandra is my mistress, and you, I believe, are named Neale or Reeve."

"Reeve," he responds, the winning smile back in position. "Charmed to make your acquaintance."

"No, you're not," I say, folding my arms across my chest. "You're standing there thinking that I'm too blunt and too forward and too plain — well, that's what I'm told people usually think of me. But that's okay. I know how to behave when I need to do so and I hate airs and graces when I don't. Remember that and we'll get along just fine."

Reeve blinks, and I see him reaching for words, but they have all flown away.

"Now, I think we need to go this way?" I say, taking pity on him. He is not the first to be rendered speechless in my presence and I suspect he will not be the last. It used to bother me that people do not like me much, but now . . . not so much. Most of the time.

I lead the way down the hallway, knowing that his good manners mean Reeve will follow.

"We?" he asks.

"I assume you're on your way to see Lorimer? I, too, have been summoned. And we're late." Glancing behind me, I catch him shaking his head. He seems to be preoccupied with my feet and I follow his gaze to my leather slippers.

They are as brown as my gown, unremarkable in any way but for the coating of dust upon them. He looks up and I meet his gaze, raising one eyebrow in challenge, but he says nothing. I will not explain to a squire why my indoor slippers are dusty – a late-night meeting of Beech Circle members in a disused cellar is not a topic for boys like him. Boys at all, really. But I make a mental note of the fact that he *noticed* the dust.

Interesting.

"Come on, then," I say, evoking deliberate lightness to break the silent tussle. "I've got a busy day ahead of me and I'd imagine that you do, too. The sooner we get this over and done with, the better."

I am at the door to Lorimer's lair, Reeve slouching along behind me, when it suddenly strikes me that if the Lady Cassandra marries Sir Garrick, I will be seeing a lot more of Reeve – and his observant eyes – in the future than I might like.

The thought is enough to still my hand mid-knock.

"Go on, then," Reeve says. "What are you waiting for?"

I pause just long enough to let him know that I will knock when I'm ready, before banging on the door.

"Enter." Lorimer's thin voice is muffled by the thick wood, but his impatience is clear. I take a deep breath, summon up Maven Who Once Appeared at Court, and push the door open, entering a room that is little larger than a cupboard.

Lorimer has furnished it with a small writing desk, polished until gleaming, and a high-backed wooden chair upholstered in a worn, striped silk that I suspect was once castle curtains. A thick green rug, also showing signs of wear, covers the floor, from corner to corner, and I note Lorimer's enterprise at having had it cut down to fit the space.

Then again, he always was enterprising.

"Ah, Maven of Aramoor," Lorimer says, and I do not flinch, even as I feel Reeve start in surprise beside me. "It is good to see you again after so many years."

I peek at Reeve, who is struggling to compose his face at the steward's deference to me, a mere maid. As Lorimer greets me with a small bow, Reeve's intake of breath is just audible.

"Lorimer," I say, ensuring I use the smooth, rich tones of the lady that Lorimer knows me to be. "Always a pleasure."

It is anything but, as Lorimer well knows, but now is not the time for semantics.

"Close your mouth, boy," says Lorimer, sneering down that thin nose in Reeve's direction. "You look like a trout that's been landed."

To his credit, Reeve does as he's told, though I feel him watching proceedings closely.

"And how are your parents, my lady?" Lorimer continues, talking to me as though Reeve was not in the room. For a moment, it is as though this were true, and I am ten years old again, running to our household steward for a coin to take to the chapel for the plate.

"Last I heard, they were well," I say, giving the man a hard stare, unwilling to say more in front of a squire I've just met. "No longer in need of a master house steward such as yourself. They have been cut down to size, much as your rug has been."

For a moment the mask slips and he grimaces, but recovers a moment later.

"And now their youngest daughter has joined me here at Rennart Castle," he says, and I can see that he is enjoying my diminished circumstances. I will not give him the satisfaction of responding.

"I go where my Lady Cassandra goes," is all I say. He knows I have no agency. Not anymore.

Not ever again.

"Indeed," Lorimer responds. "How fortunate for us then that you are here. As for you . . ."

Reeve is staring at the painting over Lorimer's desk, so busy with his thoughts that he does not notice the old man's attention has turned to him. As Lorimer's heavy gray brows begin to beetle into a frown, I dig Reeve in the ribs.

"What? Yes?" Reeve blurts out, looking around wildly.

"Yes, you," says Lorimer, not appearing to have noticed the nudge. "Airl Buckthorn commented that you served well at table last night."

I hide a smile as Reeve preens.

"But that is not to say you were perfect," Lorimer goes on. "As such, you will meet me in the Great Hall after breakfast for practice."

I cannot hear the groan but I know that it is there. Reeve looks to be about my age, perhaps a year or two older, which means that he has probably spent many years learning the ins, outs, and protocols of serving at table. I have no doubt that spending another hour going through the "pour from the left, remove from the right" routine is the last thing Reeve wants. But he says nothing.

"That is not why I brought you both here this morning, however," says Lorimer, before pausing with a frown and talking almost to himself. "I wanted Neale as well, but I imagine he is with Sir Garrick, so no mind."

He fixes us both with a steely gaze. "The next few days will be both busy and fraught for all of us. As the servants of the bride and groom, it is imperative that you two – and Neale – work together to ensure the smooth facilitation of the great day."

Lorimer pauses again, seeming to grope for the right words.

"You were there last night, Reeve of Norwood," Lorimer finally continues. "You saw . . . things are not as . . . straightforward as we might wish them to be."

Now Lorimer looks at me, questions filling his eyes.

"My Lady Cassandra is . . . unsettled," I respond, keeping my tone even. "And with good reason."

"It is not our place to discuss whys, wherefores and reasons," Lorimer says, clapping his hands together as though to end the very thought. "It is enough that we acknowledge that the path to the altar may be bumpy, and that we work together to ensure that Airl Buckthorn's wishes are carried out."

I wonder what exactly Lorimer knows – or thinks he knows – but now is not the time to probe. Not without raising his suspicions. Better to say nothing.

Lorimer is cunning, as well I understand. One does not rise to his position in any household without staying abreast of exactly what goes on in that household. And one certainly does not keep that position without a good network of spies and allies peppered throughout its halls.

Where Reeve fits in to this picture I have no idea, but, until I do, the best approach is silence.

So few people understand this.

But Lorimer has not yet finished. "If you hear of anything – anything at all, the slightest whisper – from any quarter, even those closest, that might interfere with

Airl Buckthorn's plans, you are to report them to me. On the Airl's orders."

Reeve gasps, at the same time as I grasp the meaning of his words.

"You ask too much," I say, concealing my clenched hands in the folds of my skirt. "I will not spy upon my lady."

"I ask only what Airl Buckthorn asks," says Lorimer calmly, though I can see he is enjoying our reactions. "This wedding has far-reaching implications and must go ahead. Airl Buckthorn is counting on the two of you to help make that happen."

"I am not of the Airl's household," I say, my voice rising with my temper.

"Not yet," Lorimer agrees, now pacing back and forth before us, wearing new tracks on that old green rug. "But, one way or another, it will happen, and Airl Buckthorn looks favorably upon loyalty." He stops to fix me with a beady stare.

"And what of my loyalty to Lady Cassandra?" I snap, wishing I was able to pace. "What of that?" That he dare speak to me of loyalty remains unsaid.

"In three short days, Lady Cassandra will swear a promise that will bind her to this household," Lorimer says somberly, and now he stands before me, arms folded over that thin chest.

"A promise she does not wish to give," I say, unable

to help myself. Inwardly, I curse my outburst. Now is not the time to remind the Steward of the Household that the Lady Cassandra is an unwilling bride.

"Her father has promised it on her behalf, as is her father's right," says Lorimer, and his eyes are sharp as he stares down that long nose at me. "Just as your father gave you to the service of Lady Cassandra's household."

"Yes," I breathe, unable to look at him, "as my father did." My hands are so tightly clenched, I feel the strain across my shoulders.

"And you are happy in your service to the Lady Cassandra, are you not?" Lorimer continues in a singsong voice, as though talking to a frisky horse.

My glance slides sideways once more, but Reeve continues to study the painting on Lorimer's wall, and I am grateful for his consideration. This is not a conversation I want to endure with a witness, but what choice do I have?

What choice have I ever had about anything at all?

If Lorimer wants me to discuss my current position with Lady Cassandra right here, right now, then discuss it I will have to do.

"I am happy enough," I say, picking my words with care, flexing my fingers within the folds of my skirt in an attempt to sound relaxed. "The Lady Cassandra has been kind to me."

It is the truth, if only part of the story.

"Well, then," Lorimer says, sounding smug, and making me want to slap the satisfied smile from his face. "Do you see how these things work out for the best? Why will it not be so for the Lady Cassandra?"

In the long pause that follows Lorimer's words, I watch the steward's smile fade and disappear into disapproval. He is opening his pinched mouth to speak again when I finally respond.

"My Lady Cassandra has high hopes for the future."

It is all and nothing. Enough.

Lorimer appeared satisfied with Maven's words, but Reeve recognized diplomacy when he heard it. Which made Reeve wonder what the girl was hiding—and how it might impact upon him. He had been Sir Garrick's squire for less than one full day, but he already felt protective. And whether that protectiveness was entirely for the man or in part because of the future Sir Garrick offered Reeve, the feeling was enough for now.

But what to do about it?

The discussion he'd overheard between Sir Garrick and the Airl at dinner the previous evening had suggested that the knight already had qualms about his intended bride. Should Reeve report this conversation and add fuel to that fire? Or should he simply take Maven at face value and trust that all would be well?

What he had seen so far of this odd, prickly girl did not necessarily induce trust. But Reeve also knew that the wedding would ensure they spent an awful lot of time together in the future.

It would not do to create a rift on day one.

"Very well," said Lorimer, clapping his hands together to indicate the end of the subject. "I am glad we are all on the same page. You will report to me the slightest hint of gossip or innuendo that might upset the wedding plans."

"Yes, my lord steward," said Reeve, glancing across at Maven, who murmured something that sounded like assent.

And if Lorimer could not see the girl's fingers crossed behind her back as she made her promise, then Reeve certainly could.

Following Maven out into the hall moments later, Reeve noted her ramrod-straight back and the stubborn lift of her chin. How he had mistaken her for a lowly servant, he had no idea.

"Why do you wear the garb of a maidservant?" Reeve asked her, plucking at Maven's sleeve as she began to stride off down the hall.

Maven stopped and turned to him. "Because that is what I am?" she said, her expression unreadable.

Reeve stepped back. "But Lorimer worked for your family's household, Maven of Aramoor. You have an estate."

Her mouth tightened. "When I was young," Maven said. "Since then, my father has fallen on hard times and our household is no more. My father sits and drinks above the farrier's shop, an unwelcome interloper in the village that he once owned, while my mother and my sisters and I attend to the needs of the ladies to whom we are indentured."

Reeve gasped. "Indentured?"

Maven stiffened. "Well, as good as. My mother is in service to Lady Fenlon, my sister Iva dances attendance on Lady Sandalwood, Elinor is governess to the children of Lady Canold and I —"

She broke off, breathing out hard. "I am Maven of Aramoor no more, but I am the lucky one. I was sent to Lady Cassandra to serve as her companion. It is I who chooses to wear the servant's garb. It never does to forget one's place. You would do well to remember that also."

Reeve snorted. "I am a lowly squire. One day removed from a page. It is not likely that I will forget it."

Maven laughed, and Reeve was surprised by how uplifting the hearty sound was. "Ah, Reeve of Norwood, I suspect that under other circumstances we might have one day been friends, but . . ."

Her voice trailed away and, as Reeve watched, she seemed to make up her mind about something. "The

Lady Cassandra is very unhappy about the impending marriage," she confided, watching him closely.

Reeve collected his own thoughts. "I got that impression last night," he said, allowing no hint of judgment to color his words.

"I did advise her against attending dinner," Maven said with a sigh. "But she is angry and . . . stubborn."

As Maven reached out and put a hand on his arm, Reeve realized he had not heard much beyond the word "advise." Maven was speaking as though the Lady Cassandra was the much younger servant, not the other way round.

"She really does not want to marry him, you know," Maven said, her voice low.

"She has no choice," Reeve responded, and felt Maven's grip tighten for a moment before she let go, a flicker of regret on her face – but whether it was her lady's lack of choice she regretted, or her own impulse to speak to Reeve of the matter, Reeve was not sure.

"No," Maven said, stepping back and appearing to shrink a little. "No, it certainly looks that way, doesn't it?"

With those words, she turned and strode away from him, turning left at the end of the hallway to be swallowed up by the vast maze of corridors within the castle.

CHAPTER SEVEN

Reeve was still puzzling over Maven more than an hour later – a long, boring hour spent at the shoulder of Lorimer, stifling yawn after yawn as the steward took him, in excruciating detail, through everything Reeve already knew about serving at table. But Reeve had uttered not one word of complaint.

If the household steward wanted to make Reeve stand on his head beside the Airl's chair for an hour every night, then that's what Reeve would do. His goal was to become a knight, and not just any knight, but a knight who might one day fill the Knight Protector role, just as Sir Garrick did.

A knight like that would never have to leave the shores of Cartreff. He would never be sent away by his own father, across the ocean, far from everything he knew.

Reeve liked what he knew. He knew how to negotiate the world in which he'd been brought up.

With Sir Garrick Sharp's help Reeve would get even better at it. Which meant putting up with as many silverware placement sessions as Lorimer required.

And spying on Sir Garrick?

It was this thorny question, and Maven's potential role in it, that preoccupied Reeve as he walked back through the kitchen, swiping another honey cake on the way, and out into the sunshine in the castle courtyard as the chapel bells pealed for morning service.

Munching through the crispy outer layer of the cake to the light, fluffy interior, Reeve suppressed a moan of pleasure. Aside from becoming a knight, he would do all he could to stay at Rennart Castle for the cakes . . .

A small wagon rumbled past, its wooden wheels clattering on the courtyard stones, and Reeve noticed a fine layer of steam rising from the horse's back. It was chilly enough to raise a crop of goose bumps on his own arms, despite the long sleeves of his tunic.

The ringing clang of steel upon steel caught his ears, drawing his attention to the far corner of the wide courtyard where two men, stripped bare to the waist, were practicing swordplay with lightweight weapons. Making his way toward them, Reeve took great care to avoid the mounds of horse manure that dotted his path.

Still chewing on the last of his cake, Reeve arrived at the wooden fence that surrounded the practice yard, and leaned over the top rail to watch. The two men were evenly matched, trading stroke for stroke, shouting playful insults at each other to the gathering crowd's delight.

"Is that all you've got?" shouted the taller of the two men, pushing his dark hair from his eyes with a dramatic flourish. "I've seen limp rhubarb with more spine."

"Ha!" the other man, a thickset redhead, responded, blocking a potentially lethal thrust as though batting a fly. "You clearly ate too much jelly at the feast last night, given the wobbliness of your wrist this morning. I should see the wyld woman in the woods for a salve if I were you."

As he spoke, the redhead pirouetted, taking the dark-haired man by surprise as he brought the sword up and across and struck a glancing blow on his opponent's upper arm.

"Ah!" the dark-haired swordsman yelled, dropping his own weapon to clap a hand over the thin cut. "I am hit!"

Reeve gulped as the man removed his hand, holding it up for the crowd to see – a hand now covered in blood.

Reeve dropped the last vestige of his honey cake onto the stones as he pushed himself away from the fence, trying to focus on the ground, the sky . . . anywhere.

But it was no good. A tide of wooziness began to rise within him as the rushing in his ears took over. Clutching his head, Reeve edged from the practice ring, hoping that no one had noticed him, desperate to reach a secluded spot by the castle wall to sit down for a few minutes until this wretched feeling passed.

Reeve felt a hand take his arm. "There, young sir, it's all right. Breathe in and out," a woman's voice said. "Lean on me, sir, it's all right. This way."

Concentrating on staying upright, Reeve did as the melodious voice told him, leaning against the woman and going where she led. Moments later, he was pushed onto the ground in the shade of one of the great walls.

He leaned back against the rough stone, eyes closed, knowing that the light-headedness would soon pass, but inwardly cursing it.

"Well now, young sir," came the woman's voice again, and Reeve squinted up at his savior, a tall shadow between him and the bright morning sun. "And just how long have you been affected by the sight of blood like this?"

Reeve groaned. "All of my life. Less now than when I was younger, but . . ."

She laughed. "Judging by your colors there, young sir,

I'd say you were Sir Garrick's new squire, is that right?"

Reeve froze. This woman knew Sir Garrick? The wooziness in his head was joined by a rising feeling of sickness in his stomach. Sir Garrick was already questioning Airl Buckthorn's choice of Reeve as squire — if this woman told the knight that his new squire fainted at the sight of blood . . .

"Rest easy, young sir," the woman continued, seeming to read his mind. "I'll not tell. But it seems to me that you might have a small problem here, given that knights tend to trade in bloodletting."

"I —"

"Don't speak, your secret is safe with me," the woman continued, and now she moved slightly, allowing Reeve to make out her features. Her skin was burned brown by the sun and carried the wrinkles of one who smiled a lot. Her long curly hair was streaked with gray and untroubled by a comb, but she exuded calm. Reeve couldn't help but smile back at her.

"Come and see me," she said, turning to leave. "I have a tincture that might help you."

"I — but —" Reeve spluttered at her retreating back. "Who are you?"

She grinned over her shoulder at him, and laughed — the wonderful, youthful sound enough to brighten Reeve's spirits. "Why, you heard them mention the wyld woman in the woods, did you not? That's me. Myra. I'm easy to find – ask anyone."

She laughed again before adding: "Just don't tell the Airl about it. He doesn't trust the powers of plants."

By the time Reeve opened his mouth to thank her, Myra had pushed her way into the throng of people that made up everyday life in the busy castle, and was gone. Reeve leaned back against the wall once more and swallowed, looking around the courtyard as he tried to catch his breath.

Two young boys dressed in little more than rags ran past, bright-red apples in their hands, glee and anticipation in every step. Reeve wondered briefly if they'd stolen the apples, but no one else seemed to pay them any mind. The woebegone maid with the bucket under her arm; the skinny, elfin stable hand leading the prancing pony; and the stocky, blond man methodically sweeping the far corner of the courtyard all ignored the laughing boys.

Reeve decided he would ignore them, too, but he needed to get up. Sir Garrick would soon be ready for his breakfast and would not appreciate the fact that his squire was crumpled in a heap on the cobblestones. As he pushed his way slowly to his feet, Reeve sighed.

Lady Rhoswen had always told him that he'd grow out of his "little problem," and the pair of them had gone to great pains to hide it from the rest of the Harding Manor household. Lady Rhoswen had first discovered it when Reeve had dropped to the floor in her parlor one morning when she'd pierced her finger with an embroidery needle.

He was lucky, Reeve knew, that Lady Rhoswen was willing to help him, so firmly did she believe in his potential. It was one of the reasons she'd kept him in her household as long as she had, rather than sending him out, as was her right, to squire for anyone who would have him the day he'd turned fourteen.

And now it had almost all come undone on his first full day at Rennart Castle . . .

A shrill, horrified scream pierced Reeve's thoughts, and he froze. As those around him also stilled, Reeve surveyed the courtyard to try to identify where the scream had come from.

As another earsplitting shriek rent the air, Reeve realized the sound was coming from one of the high windows of the castle keep – the inner sanctum and residence that rose above the central courtyard. A restless murmur filled the air around him, though nobody moved.

"Help!" howled the voice. "It's gone! It's gone! Stolen! Help!"

To Reeve's horror, the Lady Cassandra, hair in disarray, appeared at the window, wildly waving her bare arms and apparently wearing just her shift, though the casement hid most of her body.

"It's gone!" she wailed again, across the courtyard, and the people standing near Reeve gasped as one. "The Fire Star! It's been stolen!"

"Tell us again, my dear. Exactly as you remember it."

The Lady Cassandra sniffed. "Uncle, I have been over it and over it."

"Once more," the Airl said, and Reeve couldn't have said if his tone was cajoling or commanding.

Lady Cassandra sighed. "I awoke this morning, Maven brought me tea in my bed, as always, then assisted me to the dressing table to begin our morning routine. The Fire Star had been placed in its own pouch last night and tucked into my jewelry case, as always — I saw it. When we opened the case this morning to extract the green earbobs that Maven had decided would best complement today's gown, we discovered that the pouch containing the Fire Star was missing."

Airl Buckthorn said nothing, tapping his quill on the vellum in front of him. He had called Sir Garrick to his solar as soon as word of the Fire Star's disappearance had reached him. Reeve, who had rushed straight to Sir Garrick's rooms from the courtyard, had managed only to blurt out to the bleary-eyed knight that the Fire Star was gone when Lorimer had arrived at the door with the Airl's summons.

Of Neale there had still been no sign.

Once Lorimer had left to oversee a search for the stone, Reeve had assisted Sir Garrick to dress and offered to follow him to the Airl's solar with breakfast — an arrangement with which Sir Garrick had gratefully acquiesced.

And so it was that Reeve, who had delivered to Sir Garrick a trencher of poached fruits and had positioned himself as inconspicuously as possible near the door, was now able to witness firsthand the Lady Cassandra's story. Maven, he noticed, was also here, though she hadn't acknowledged Reeve's presence with so much as a blink. In her maid's dress of brown, she almost blended in to the walls.

Appalled as he was by the disappearance of the Fire Star, Reeve was also intrigued. That such a magnificent stone had been stolen not only from under the noses of the Lady Cassandra and her maid, but within the walls of one of the most powerful men in the kingdom, was a major puzzle — and, potentially, a scandal from which the House of Buckthorn would find it difficult to recover.

"Right now, the castle is being turned upside down," said the Airl. "If that stone is hidden within these walls, Lorimer will find it."

"And if it's not?" demanded Lady Cassandra. "What

then, my lord? I had thought that my family's greatest asset would be safe within my uncle's home."

"We will find it," the Airl reiterated, and Reeve shuddered at the steel in his tone. Woe betide anyone found to be holding that stone. "But for now, we must continue with the wedding plans."

"Bah!" said Lady Cassandra, and Reeve's eyes widened at her most unladylike expression. "As if I can focus on trussing myself up like a turkey when this has happened. If you cannot return the stone to me, I will not walk down the aisle."

Airl Buckthorn glowered at his niece. "You will do as your father expressly bids you to do. Else you will bear the consequences."

"Bah!" Lady Cassandra said again, her shoulders heaving. Reeve could not see her face clearly, but he could see her hands clenching and the straightness of her spine. "The nunnery? You would send me there? You would do that to your own flesh and blood?"

"Your father and I have a contract," Airl Buckthorn said, standing up to thump on his desk.

Sir Garrick was impassive beside the Airl, but Reeve thought he detected the knight wincing at the Airl's words. Reeve had not seen Airl Buckthorn on the battlefield, but he had a fearsome reputation as a ruthless man. He was regarded as a man who would do everything within his power to uphold the laws of the kingdom and protect what he thought was right – but also protect what was his.

Reeve decided he would not wish to have the Airl's fearsome power directed at him.

The Lady Cassandra, however, appeared to have no such qualms. "That contract specifically mentions the Fire Star," she said, trying, but not quite succeeding, in sounding bored. "But it seems that someone in this household wants that stone even more than you do, Uncle."

"That stone is mine," Airl Buckthorn bellowed, thumping a fist on his desk. "I will have it for Anice."

"The Fire Star is not yours yet," the Lady Cassandra countered, hands on hips. "It will not be in your keeping until my husband decrees that I must present it to your daughter. And it seems that fate has decided it will not be yours at all."

"Indeed, it seems that greedy hands conspire to divert the course of true love," said Airl Buckthorn, his jaw tight, as Reeve puzzled over Lady Cassandra's other words. "And for this reason I will place the search for the Fire Star into the hands of the one who has the most to lose should it not be returned."

He turned to Sir Garrick, standing by his side. "Garrick, I charge you with unearthing the culprit of this terrible crime and returning the stone to its rightful owner."

Sir Garrick nodded.

"And," said Airl Buckthorn, "I should begin with those who are most recently resident in this castle."

Reeve quailed as the Airl's gaze fell upon him. "You," said Airl Buckthorn, pointing a finger at Reeve. "Where were you last night and this morning?"

"I, er, I put Sir Garrick to bed after dinner and then I —" Reeve paused, remembering his long walk through the darkened hallways of the castle — and the shadowy figure that had rushed headlong into him.

"Then?" asked Airl Buckthorn, leaning forward on his desk.

"I went to my own rooms," said Reeve, trying to untangle his thoughts. "This morning, I went to the kitchens and saw Lorimer and —"

"And?" Airl Buckthorn prompted. "Stop dithering, boy. All of this pausing and groping for words is making you look more and more guilty."

"Well, I went out to the courtyard to watch the sword practice . . ." The very thought of it made his head swim all over again and, for a moment, Reeve worried he might faint right here. "Then —"

A picture of the woman, Myra, appeared before him. What was the wyld woman from the woods doing in the courtyard that morning, anyway? And where had she disappeared to so abruptly? Yet she'd been so friendly to him . . .

Airl Buckthorn's brows were knitted together. "Then?"

"Then, the Lady Cassandra started screaming and, well, here I am."

"Plenty of opportunity for him to have had something to do with this!" the Lady Cassandra shrieked, and Reeve swallowed again. It was true that there were times when he'd been on his own, but surely she couldn't think that he would have taken her gemstone?

Reeve risked a glance at Maven, but she was looking only at Lady Cassandra.

"Now, now," said Sir Garrick, holding his hands up as he stepped forward. "Reeve is the newest member of our household, and the timing of his arrival is inopportune, but the Lady Rhoswen holds him in high esteem. I cannot believe . . ."

He turned back to Reeve. "Do you swear that you had nothing to do with this crime?"

Reeve swallowed. "On everything I hold dear."

"Hmmm," said Airl Buckthorn, one eyebrow raised at his Knight Protector. "While the Lady Rhoswen has told me she believes the boy to be clever and observant — and on that we shall see — at this time we have no suspects for the robbery. Therefore, as the newest resident of the castle, the weight of suspicion is upon him."

Airl Buckthorn paused, staring up at the ceiling for a moment, deep in thought, before turning back to Reeve.

"I charge you, then, to prove us wrong. You will assist Sir Garrick in his inquiries. You have only a few days to find that gemstone and unmask the true culprit. If you cannot do this, I'm afraid that you must bear the brunt of failure and will be sent home to your parents in disgrace."

Reeve could barely think. Airl Buckthorn was more or less admitting that he knew it wasn't Reeve who had stolen the stone, but was also letting him know that someone was going to have to take the blame – and that someone would be Reeve if he could not assist Sir Garrick in finding the true thief!

Failure meant the end of his dream to become a knight, for no one would take him on as a squire ever again.

Failure meant the end of ever proving to his father that Reeve was not a poor copy of Larien.

Failure would mean certain passage for Reeve on a ship bound for parts unknown.

There was a deep silence in the room as Reeve tried to formulate an answer. He glanced again at Maven, who had not moved during the entire exchange, but she continued to ignore him. Reeve could feel Airl Buckthorn's attention upon him like a yoke, and hear his own breathing in his ears.

In desperation, Reeve risked a look at Sir Garrick.

To his surprise, the knight directed a very tiny, barely discernible nod at him.

Heartened by the knight's support, Reeve lifted his chin. With right on his side, and Sir Garrick to help him, surely he would be able to bring the true perpetrator of the crime to light.

"I accept your terms, your excellency," Reeve said, knowing that, really, he had no choice in the matter. "I did not do this thing, and welcome the opportunity to help bring the thief to justice."

Airl Buckthorn inclined his head. "Very well," he said, as though accepting a generous offer of assistance rather than the answer to a threat. "You may start immediately. Garrick, where will you begin?"

"In the lady's rooms, my lord, if she is willing to allow us access," Sir Garrick said.

Lady Cassandra did not hesitate. "Of course," she said. "Though what you expect to find there, I have no idea. It is what is *not* there that is important. Maven, take them."

Maven sketched a small curtsey to Sir Garrick before walking toward the door. "This way, sire."

Following the knight from the room, Reeve felt the honey cake he'd eaten that morning churning inside him. He could scarcely believe how quickly his life had changed. In the past day, he'd gone from a home he'd known and loved at Harding Manor into the turmoil of life at Rennart Castle. In the process, he'd gone from petted page of Lady Rhoswen into the second squire of a man who didn't even seem to want his services.

And now to this.

If he could not help Sir Garrick to track down the Fire Star and its thief, Airl Buckthorn would lay the blame solely at Reeve's feet, and send him back to his parents and the banishment that would result.

CHAPTER EIGHT

Lady Cassandra has always been a violent sleeper. I watch Reeve avert his gaze from the crumpled sheets and untucked blankets beneath the deep-blue curtains of the bed's canopy. With a blush, he turns his attention instead to the still-open window, through which I can hear the ringing clang of the blacksmith's hammer. Indeed, the courtyard below hums with the bustle of normal life, quite as though nothing has happened.

The wispy white curtains dance gently in the light breeze, and I can see dots of dust, like starbursts, floating in the shafts of morning sunlight.

"What do you see?" Sir Garrick asks, and Reeve turns

to him with a frown as I steady my breathing, drawing in the faint scent of lavender.

"Don't be a dullard," says Sir Garrick, snapping his fingers. "When we track prey in the forest, or try to outwit enemies across the countryside, the key is to focus on exactly what you can see, what you can hear, what you can smell. Not what you *think* you should see or hear or smell."

I shudder a little at the analogy of the hunt. It will not do to underestimate this man, and Lady Cassandra must never forget it.

Reeve stands to attention, his head leaning to the right as he studies the room. I stand silently at my post, as still as one of the Airl's stone statues.

"Say it aloud, boy," Sir Garrick says, watching Reeve with those fierce black eyes. "Let us see if we agree."

"Very well," says Reeve, and I can see the effort it takes him to think in the face of Sir Garrick's intense observation. Much is at stake for this new squire, and he will want to impress.

"The window is open, but whether that is because it was open all night or because Lady Cassandra opened it to sound the alarm this morning, I do not . . ."

Reeve stops, appearing to think hard. "I think it was open already. I was in the courtyard and did not hear the shutters slam against the stone before I heard the scream, nor after."

My heart sinks at his words, but I keep my expression blank.

Sir Garrick's forehead smooths. "Very good," he says. "Very good indeed. Go on."

Reeve creeps forward, avoiding the dressing table, peering at the floor. "I can see many footprints in the rug," he says, his hands mimicking the way in which the fibers of the thick rug have been disturbed. "They are . . ."

Reeve pauses again, kneeling down beside the disturbed section of the rug. "There is one bare foot – I can see the toes. The Lady Cassandra, recently alighted from her bed, perhaps?"

"And?" Sir Garrick prompts.

"One pair of soft house shoes, of around the same size as the bare foot," Reeve continues, glancing across the short distance from the open window to the dresser. "And one larger, dusty shoe print – no, boot print."

Reeve crawls over to take a closer look at the boot print. "Strange."

"What's strange?" says Sir Garrick, and now he moves across the room to stand beside Reeve as my mouth goes dry. "What?"

"There is just the one boot print," says Reeve. "And it's facing toward the window."

"And that's strange because?" Sir Garrick queries.

"Well," says Reeve, standing to examine the windowsill, careful to avoid the boot print. "If someone had climbed in the window, I would think there would be at least one other boot print, with the toes pointing into the room. But just one, facing out of the room is . . . strange."

I inwardly curse him.

"Not strange," says Sir Garrick, "if the thief was already inside the castle and made his escape out of the window." I almost let out a sigh of relief, but manage to contain myself.

"True," Reeve agrees, leaning out through the window to stare down to the courtyard below. "But it's a long way down, with few toeholds in the stone. If he managed to creep in without waking Lady Cassandra, why would he not sneak out the same way?"

I am back to silently cursing. He is altogether too clever for his own good, this squire.

But I am more than a match for him. I move to stand beside Reeve at the window.

"Perhaps he was surprised," I say, deliberately placing my foot into the disturbed section of the rug, all the better to mess it up some more. "I sleep in my lady's dressing room, and I wake very early. As you saw this morning."

Reeve pulls back, resting his hands on the sill as we both stare out across the great courtyard. A plump milkmaid leads a huge brown cow past a group of young men who are lounging on hay bales near the stables, lazing in the morning sun. I recognize the rowdy group that filed past me into the hallway last night.

"And yet," says Reeve, slowly, "you mentioned no intruder, and neither did the lady?"

I swallow before responding as calmly as possible. "Just because I did not see him does not mean I did not surprise him."

Reeve turns his head to give me a long look, and I return his gaze without wavering.

"I have seen enough here," says Sir Garrick, breaking the deadlock, and gesturing for Reeve to follow. "It seems that our thief was a member of the household, and so we have only to wait for Lorimer to unearth the stolen goods and all shall be revealed."

"But —" Reeve continues to stare down at the courtyard, appearing to search for someone, before remembering his place and walking toward the door.

"Enough," Sir Garrick reiterates, opening the door to the hallway. "I understand that you are under some pressure with regard to this, but rest assured that Airl Buckthorn would not have set you this task if he did not truly think that unmasking the thief would be the work of minutes. Leave it to Lorimer."

Reeve pauses mid step. "Sire, I could assist Lorimer," he begins, his face looking worried. I understand his worry and, for a moment, feel bad for him. After all, if the thief is not unmasked, it is Reeve who gets the blame and is sent home.

But feeling sorry for him does not mean that I will help him. Every hour that the Fire Star remains missing is one hour closer to freedom for Lady Cassandra. And for me.

Sir Garrick laughs, pulling me from my thoughts. "How? A mere boy? Lorimer is a thorough man, and a splendid steward. If anyone can winkle out the truth, he can."

He pauses, seeming to really look at Reeve's anxious face for the first time. "Well," he says, "I can see how this means a great deal to you. If it would help you to feel as though you are doing something, then ask any questions you can get away with. But be aware that most will not even speak to you. You are too new to be useful to anyone just yet."

With that cursory summary of castle life, Sir Garrick steps out into the hallway, his voice floating back through the door. "I will expect to see you at lunch. Do not be late."

After Sir Garrick's departure, the room felt strangely silent to Reeve, despite, or perhaps because of, Maven's presence. Under the girl's disquieting gaze, Reeve continued to pace the room, noting as he did that Lady Cassandra's traveling trunks were all in a neat pile in the far corner of the room. The door to the dressing room was shut, but Reeve could imagine that the Lady Cassandra's gowns, including her wedding attire, were all laid out inside.

It seemed that Maven had been busy.

Reeve paused, looking at the closed door. Something about it bothered him, but he couldn't put a finger on what it was.

Reeve took a step toward it.

"Is there something I can help you with?" Maven asked. "You seem to have more questions?"

Reeve paused at the dressing room door, which seemed to taunt him. Without responding to her question, he turned the brass knob, pushed the door open and looked inside.

To his disappointment, it was as tidy and ordinary as the room he'd just left. The Lady Cassandra's gowns — three of them — were hanging on hooks on the walls, airing. They had few creases in them, which spoke to careful packing at the beginning of her journey. One of the gowns was shrouded in a light muslin cloth, stamped on the outside with a simple drawing of a tree and a tiny red bird — Lady Cassandra's wedding finery, Reeve assumed, wondering which of the kingdom's finest seamstresses had stamped this mark, which he did not recognize, on the overlay.

Two leather cases, straps buckled, sat on the floor beneath the shrouded gown, and three pairs of shoes were lined, toes to the wall, beside them. On the opposite side of the narrow room, beneath a tall stained glass window, lay a thin mattress, the quilts pulled up to the pillow.

"Getting an eyeful, are you?"

Reeve turned toward the voice behind him. Maven had moved and now leaned, unsmiling, on the wall near the door.

"You don't talk like any lady I've ever heard," Reeve blurted out. He'd done nothing wrong here but, somehow, this girl made him feel as though he'd been snooping.

Maven grimaced. "And how many 'ladies' have you actually spoken to? Besides people who have to be nice to you, that is."

"I, er, well —" Reeve could feel his face getting hotter and hotter. It was true that most of his interactions with girls had been in practice sessions for etiquette and chivalry. Except for . . .

"The Lady Anice," he blurted out. "She's never nice to me."

"Hmmm," said Maven, prowling across the room toward him like a cat surveying a field mouse. "Well, that makes you just one of many."

"You know her?" Reeve asked, surprised, willing his feet not to take a step backward.

Maven stopped in front of him, unsmiling. "I do."

Reeve waited for more details, but she said nothing.

"Right, well, er, I'd best be off then," Reeve said, moving to walk around her.

"I heard what was said this morning," Maven said, suddenly, putting a hand on his arm. "I know what's at stake for you. But don't think for one moment that I will allow the Lady Cassandra to be hurt because you want to be a knight."

Reeve took in her words, controlling his expression with effort. "All I want is the same as she does," he said, perplexed. "The truth about what happened to the Fire Star. Surely, getting it back is what she needs?"

"Indeed," Maven said after a tiny beat. "But she is a pawn in this game of men and she deserves better. She does not feel safe here."

Reeve just managed to stop a snort. "She is safe with Sir Garrick. There is no better knight in the kingdom."

Maven dropped her hand and stepped back, allowing Reeve to pass. "That's as may be," she said. "But the Fire Star was here for just one night, and it has been spirited away. It would take a well-connected person with great strategic skills to plan a robbery on such short notice."

Reeve gasped, stepping back in shock. "You are not suggesting that Sir Garrick had anything to do with this?" Had this girl taken leave of her senses?

Maven paused, her face solemn. "I am not," she said, finally, and Reeve let out a breath he hadn't realized he'd been holding. "But everyone knows that he is as lukewarm about this marriage as my lady is. If he has the Fire Star, he doesn't need to marry her to get it – and everyone knows that the only reason he is marrying is because Airl Buckthorn wants that stone."

Reeve felt his eyebrows knit together. "You are suggesting that Sir Garrick and the Airl have conspired to steal the Fire Star? But that makes no sense! You heard Lorimer this morning – Airl Buckthorn wants this marriage to go ahead at all costs."

Maven tossed her hair. "All I'm saying is that the stone is one of the most valuable in the kingdom. It is Lady Cassandra's greatest asset. Without it, she is reduced to ruins, and any chance at future happiness is gone. She will go to the nunnery."

Reeve hesitated, mulling over what Maven had said. A thought struck him. "And you? Where will you go if she goes to the nunnery?"

"Why, with her, of course," said Maven, her pointed chin lifted. "As her companion, I will join Lady Cassandra in the cloister."

Reeve was careful not to meet her eyes. He couldn't imagine spending the rest of his life locked up behind high walls, giving his days over to prayer and contemplation, and, from what he'd seen of Maven, even after such a short time, he could not imagine her in the role of supplicant novice, either.

"If I unearth the thief and find the stone, I am able to help us all," he said.

"Perhaps," Maven said, moving past him to the window at the end of the dressing room. "Perhaps."

Reeve bowed toward her. "Then I will leave you now," he said. "There is much to do and not much time in which to do it."

"Less than three days," Maven said softly, still staring through the glass.

CHAPTER NINE

Finding the Fire Star in a place the size of Rennart Castle, with its rabbit warren of rooms, countless nooks and crannies, plus secret passages that even the very old struggled to remember, was always going to be difficult. As Reeve stared out over the Great Hall, now packed to bursting with the Lady Cassandra's entourage along with the keenest wedding guests, he began to wonder if Airl Buckthorn had only set him the task to get rid of him.

There were upward of two hundred people in the hall for luncheon, on top of the one hundred or so servants that he knew were going about their daily business of keeping the castle running — with another two hundred guests to come before the wedding day. As he stood behind Sir Garrick's chair, ready to tend to the knight's every need, Reeve's mind spun at the size of the task ahead of him.

To Reeve's right, Lord Harrenth, the Lady Cassandra's father, sat deep in conversation with Airl Buckthorn, his expression pained. Lord Harrenth had arrived before lunch, full of bluster and bad mood after his discovery that Lady Cassandra had taken it upon herself to steal away from his home and arrive at Rennart Castle the day before. The bad mood escalated into apoplexy at the news of the Fire Star's disappearance.

Reeve knew the Airl had convinced the man to cause no fuss about the theft for the moment, but the strain it was placing on their relationship was clear.

Sir Garrick sat in silence, chewing his roast boar methodically, and Reeve could almost hear the cogs whirling in his brain.

"Reeve," he said suddenly, not turning to face his squire, "tell me again about that boot print. Quietly."

Reeve leaned forward, as though responding to a request, and poured ale from a silver jug into Sir Garrick's tankard. "One boot print, facing the window," Reeve whispered.

Sir Garrick took a slow sip from the tankard. "And it struck you as odd?"

"It did," Reeve affirmed, taking his time as he placed the jug back on the table.

"As it did I," said Sir Garrick. He wiped his lips with a linen cloth. "Go now to the courtyard, under that window. Report back to me directly after lunch on what you see."

Reeve swallowed. "I am dismissed from table?" he asked, knowing it would not reflect well that he was being sent away before the meal ended.

Sir Garrick caught his eye and smiled. "Do not fear. I shall tell the Airl you were on my business."

Reeve bowed low and retreated from the table before ducking toward the door.

Outside the great hall, the hallway buzzed with activities as servants strode in the doors with platters of food and out of them with trays of dirty trenchers. Weaving through the hustle, Reeve followed a maidservant with a platter piled high with food scraps down toward the steamy kitchen, then darted past the door as Cook shouted orders, making for the side door that led him out into the sunny courtyard.

Reeve took a moment to fill his lungs with fresh air, a relief after the smoky closeness of the Great Hall where a fire roared day and night, no matter what the season, due to the chill created by its stone walls and vast proportions. With most castle residents inside for luncheon, the courtyard was a subdued place, and it was so quiet that Reeve fancied he could hear the honeybees buzzing through the tall spears of lavender that were planted along the border of the walled kitchen garden.

The soft burble of voices beyond the wall caught his ear. Reeve slowed, wondering who would be wandering through the knot garden now, when all the kitchen staff were working so hard to keep everyone fed. He walked past the wooden gate, then hesitated.

His curiosity had gotten him into trouble one too many times when he was younger – first from his brother, who'd hated him for "spying," then from some of the residents of Harding Manor, who had complained he was always underfoot.

But this was different.

This time, he was tasked by the Airl to find the Fire Star, and surely that meant that he needed to investigate anything that might pertain to that matter?

Torn, Reeve stood with his hand on the gate, listening.

He heard a girl's soft giggle, and the rumbling tones of a man's voice in response.

The girl protested with a laugh, though Reeve was unable to hear her words clearly, and the man's voice came again, this time wheedling.

Reeve dropped his hand from the gate. This was not his business. It was just a servant girl and her beau taking the opportunity for a clandestine meeting.

He turned to leave.

"Brantley, no!" came the girl's voice again, still laughing but this time more commanding, and Reeve suddenly heard her footsteps striding toward the gate. Not wanting to be seen — particularly when he'd decided *not* to spy — Reeve tucked himself in behind a lavender shrub, hoping the bees wouldn't mind some company.

The gate swung open as the girl giggled again. "I decide when you get a kiss," she said as she stepped through, and Reeve caught a glimpse of swirling red hair and a bronze-colored velvet gown. "Never forget that."

As the girl looked right and left, smoothing her curls, Reeve shrank back against the wall, biting his lip as he recognized Lady Anice.

Now, Anice skipped lightly away around the side of the castle, ignoring the servants' entrance that Reeve had used to enter the courtyard. Moments later, the tall, slightly unkempt form of Brantley slouched out behind her, a sly grin spreading across his face.

"We'll see about that, my lady," he muttered, with a nasty emphasis on "lady." "We'll see who's boss very, very soon."

Reeve waited several long moments after Brantley ambled off toward the stables before emerging from his scented hiding place. As he scurried across the courtyard, he tried to push what he'd just seen from his mind.

If the Lady Anice ever found out what he'd just witnessed, his life would not be worth living.

"There was nothing beneath the window, sire," Reeve reported to Sir Garrick a short time later. Reeve had examined the area beneath the Lady Cassandra's window, not really knowing what he was looking for, before scarpering to the Knight Protector's rooms to await his presence. Fortunately, Sir Garrick had managed to extricate himself from the luncheon relatively quickly, despite being its star attraction.

"You looked closely," Sir Garrick stated, as though Reeve would have done any less.

"Of course, sire," said Reeve, trying not to sound affronted. "The area beneath the window had been swept —"

"Swept?" Sir Garrick leaned forward in his dark, carved-wood chair. "Swept when?"

"I, well, I —" Reeve paused. "There was a man near there with a broom this morning when the Lady Cassandra screamed . . . I saw him."

"Before the scream or after?" Sir Garrick inquired.

"Before," said Reeve. "It was because of the boys."

"Boys?" Sir Garrick prompted.

"Two boys with apples," said Reeve, closing his eyes to try to picture the scene in his mind. "I was sitting —"

"Sitting where? And why? Surely my squires do not

have time to simply sit!"

Reeve felt his face go hot, remembering why he had been sitting observing the boys. "It was only for a moment," he blustered, rushing on with the story as furrows began to appear along Sir Garrick's forehead. "But the point is, I saw the man sweeping along that wall, and then I heard the scream."

Sir Garrick sat back in his seat. "What did the sweeping man do?"

"I, er, I don't know," said Reeve, trying to concentrate. "There was a scream, everyone turned toward it, the Lady Cassandra was there and then . . ."

"And then? Think, boy!" Sir Garrick said.

Reeve turned his gaze to the painted ceiling as though the intricate hatched pattern between the beams might inspire his memory to greater effort. To his surprise, it seemed to work, as the morning's events flooded back to him and he could picture the scene: the screaming, the gasps of horror and then . . .

"Everyone rushed inside!" he said. "It was like they just wanted to get closer but . . ."

"But?"

"Most went toward the kitchen, which is actually *further* from the window."

"The sweeping man?" Sir Garrick probed. "He went, too?"

"I don't know," Reeve admitted. "But I know someone

who might." Even as he spoke, Reeve wished he could take the words back, remembering Myra's smiling face – and her last warning to him about the Airl not finding out about her visit.

There was a pause. "Well?" said Sir Garrick. "Must I guess or are you going to share this mystery witness with me?"

"I –" Reeve's thoughts raced. He believed Myra might have witnessed something in the courtyard, but he also didn't want to get her into any trouble. Not when she had been so kind to him.

Not when she knew his secret.

"I don't remember," Reeve murmured, his ears burning as the older man looked at him askance.

"You don't remember who may or may not have witnessed something important pertaining to the theft of the Fire Star," said Sir Garrick.

Reeve took a minute, trying to look as though he was considering his response. "Er, no."

Sir Garrick stood up, pacing his sitting room, tossing a silver coin up and down in one hand. "It seems that Lady Rhoswen was sadly wrong about your usefulness," he said. "It is just a shame that she is not here to take responsibility for her terrible misjudgment. Or perhaps it is a good thing she is not here to see it."

Reeve swallowed. "My Lady Rhoswen has not arrived?"

Sir Garrick tossed the coin in the air. "Your Lady Rhoswen has been detained by illness and will not, it seems, make the wedding after all. I've a good mind to tell the Airl how useless your investigations have been thus far, and send you back to Harding Manor to empty her chamber pot."

On the last words, Sir Garrick turned to stare intently at Reeve. "Unless, as I posit, you know more than you are willing to tell. Trying to protect someone, methinks. Some young maid you were perhaps 'sitting' with? Is that right, Reeve of Norwood?"

Reeve stared at his feet as he chewed the inside of his cheek. If he agreed with Sir Garrick's theory, he would be seen as a lovesick layabout. If he did not agree, he would look addle-headed.

After a moment, Reeve nodded miserably, and Sir Garrick sighed.

"Very well, I will give you until nightfall to speak to your 'someone' and see if you can learn more. If you do, you can stay. If not, the Airl will be updated on just how little you do know, and it will be up to him whether you go back to Harding Manor or home to your parents."

Reeve lifted his head, feeling hopeful, but Sir Garrick had already moved to his desk. "On your way out, take this wedding seating plan to Lorimer and tell him that I don't care where he puts the Baron of Brenland as long as it's as far from me as possible."

Accepting the scroll from Sir Garrick's outstretched hand, Reeve backed out of the room before half running down the hallway. He had just hours to speak to Myra and hope she had some new piece of information to impart.

But first, he had to find her . . .

"And just where do you think you're going?"

Freezing mid step, Reeve just managed to suppress a groan as Lorimer's voice cracked like a brittle whip behind him. Having arrived to discover the steward's office empty, Reeve had left the seating plan on the desk with a scrawled note before making for the courtyard. He'd made it as far as the door.

Now, swallowing his impatience, Reeve composed his face before turning to face the older man — who was accompanied by a bemused Maven.

"Have you no duties to attend to, Reeve of Norwood?" Lorimer continued, arms folded. "In Neale's confounding absence, Sir Garrick's chambers require attention."

"Sir Garrick has sent me on an errand," said Reeve, not wishing to say more in front of Maven.

Lorimer's brow arched upward. "An errand of what nature?"

"A personal nature," Reeve responded, staring straight at Lorimer. He knew if he wavered now, the steward would take him back to his office and the next hour might be wasted on infernal questions. An hour Reeve could ill afford.

"Hmmm," tutted Lorimer, lips pursed as though undecided whether to probe further.

"The good sir knight must have much to organize," inserted Maven in an unexpected show of support that took Reeve by surprise. "The wedding night will be upon us any moment."

Lorimer cleared his throat, while Reeve tried to imagine just what it was he, a lowly squire, could possibly be in charge of for a wedding night. Fortunately, he was saved from responding.

"Be off with you then," Lorimer said. "Don't keep Sir Garrick waiting. And report back here the minute your, er, personal errand is completed."

Reeve didn't hesitate, hurrying toward the door before Lorimer could change his mind, and dashing out into the bright sunlight of the courtyard.

Deep in thought, Reeve made his way across to the castle's high iron gates.

CHAPTER TEN

Where can he possibly be going, this squire with a mission? My lady has given me leave today to observe his movements, among other things, but I did not expect that Reeve would leave the walls of Rennart Castle — and especially not at the same time as I must do so. Perhaps I should have let Lorimer have Reeve . . . But no. Even I would not be so cruel when he seemed so desperate to get away.

Does he think he will find the Fire Star lying on the road? I can only hope that the hot sun and thin soles of his boots conspire to send him back toward the castle sooner rather than later. It will not do for him to reach the bottom of the hill.

I have no fear of the world outside the walls, but I wonder if Reeve knows how much of a target he is with that blue fox on his chest. There are many who would seek to settle a score with the Knight Protector by picking off an unaccompanied squire – and some who care only that he resides in comfort at Rennart Castle while they do not.

I fade behind a tree as Reeve pauses, looking right and left into the woods on either side of the dusty road. Thanks to the castle's lofty position at the top of the hill, I am above him with a clear view down the road to the patchwork of green pastures below.

In the halls of Rennart Castle, I have observed how Reeve moves with skill, weaving through the throngs with an adroit step, a practiced smile and an uncanny ability to read a room. Interesting that once the crowds of people disappear, so too does any cunning he has.

Shaking my head, I follow him as he blunders along and peers into the trees, always searching, unaware of the dangers that may lurk in the shadows. Anyone lying in wait for passing opportunity – and there are many in these times, when people are driven to desperation by hunger and despair while our King and his friends eat fifteen courses off solid-gold plates – will have due notice of his presence and ample time to prepare an ambush.

Suddenly, Reeve darts across the road and I tense, pulling out the small knife I keep concealed in the deep pockets of my skirt, unsheathing it in one motion from its leather case. The knife was a parting gift from my father as he sold me into my current position for the price of a gambling debt, exhorting me to "protect my honor," even as he extinguished his own.

There have been several occasions when I have been glad not only of its presence, but of the many lonely hours I have spent in learning to use it with precision. It is surprisingly satisfying to hit a target from five, ten, even twenty paces, and incredibly reassuring to know where best to thrust a blade for maximum impact.

The Beech Circle teaches its members to do more than talk and support each other. For we have all seen what happens when base instincts overcome civility and when speeches cannot resurrect good sense.

We know that there comes a time when action is all that is left.

Gripping the wooden handle now, I watch Reeve, unsure whether he is breaking away from something that has startled him in the woods or running toward something that has caught his attention on the other side of the road.

When he stops and stands, staring open-mouthed at a patch of brambles, I realize it is the latter, so I stash my knife carefully back in my pocket. Affecting a casual stroll, I wander down the hill, Reeve's stillness alerting me to his shock.

To my surprise, he suddenly slaps one hand over his mouth and reels back like a drunkard. I run to him, grabbing his arm before he falls onto the road.

"Are you all right? What's wrong?" There is a worrying, green tinge to Reeve's face.

"I'm fine," he gasps, and I lower him to a seated position in the dust, watching as he puts his head between his knees. As Reeve draws in huge, shaky breaths, I turn my attention to the bramble patch and what it is that might have brought on this reaction.

It takes a moment for my gaze to penetrate the thick, prickly foliage, but then I see it. And "it" almost has me sitting on the road beside Reeve.

One fixed brown eye peers at me through the tangled leaves and wiry branches, above a flash of scarlet tunic. As my sight adjusts, I make out blond hair, the pale oval of a face – and the blood dripping across the nose and down into the earth.

"Oh no," I moan, reaching forward to clear a patch in the brambles, and my worst fears are realized. "It cannot be."

"It's the sweeping man," Reeve says, sounding faint. "I think he's dead. I saw the red and –"

"Oh no," I moan again, interrupting his babble, now dragging brambles from the body, patting it down as I go. "Oh no."

"You keep saying that," says Reeve, and his face seems

to be returning to a normal color as his curiosity rises. "Did you know him?"

"No!" I snap instinctively, my mind reeling as I realize that the body has been relieved of everything but his clothes. "Of course not!" I try to sound truthful but I know my voice trembles.

Reeve stares at me for a long moment. "I don't think I believe you," he says. "Did you know that you nod every time you say no? And you are upset about something . . ."

"I'm —" I look down into his blue eyes, which are dark with concern. "I'm —"

"Maven, something is wrong. Let me help you." He reaches for my hand, and I register that he is speaking to me as though I am a saddle-shy horse.

"I need to find that stone as much as you do," Reeve continues, and the spell is broken.

"Stone?" I say, taking back my hand as I bluster. "What has this to do with the Fire Star?"

Reeve sighs. "Why else would you be out here following me down the road? Why else were you as jumpy as a cat when Sir Garrick was searching your rooms? It's clear to me you know more about what's going on than you should." By now, he has pulled himself up to stand on shaky legs.

"Then why are you out here?" I challenge, ignoring an impulse to offer an arm for support. "If you're so sure I'm involved, why didn't you tell Lorimer?"

"All I want is the stone back," Reeve says, dusting off his hands. "If I don't find it, I'll never be a knight, and I want more than anything in the whole world to be a knight. But when you told me about the nunnery . . ."

"We're not going to a nunnery," I say, staring at him, hating the direction this whole conversation has taken. "She's not marrying Sir Garrick but we are *not* going to any nunnery."

"So, what was the plan then? This man steals the Fire Star, then, once the wedding guests arrive and the castle is in chaos, you steal away, collect the stone and the pair of you go . . . Where? Across the water to Talleben?"

"What a lovely story you weave –" I begin, hoping my alarm is well hidden. Was it only minutes ago I used the word "blundering" in connection with this squire? How I wish he had left that astute mind in the castle.

"Do not take me for a fool, my lady," he interjects. Reeve's tone is mild, but in his voice I hear years of training at the knee of Lady Rhoswen.

I have met the Lady Rhoswen only once, but her reputation for good sense is impressive – a fact I have never been able to reconcile against the reality of her daughter, Anice.

Cassandra has always maintained that Anice, whose company I tolerated on several memorable occasions in my former life and whose presence I now must endure, is the product of Airl Buckthorn's indulgence rather than Lady Rhoswen's acumen.

How strange it is to me that a man so hardened to battle is so soft with his daughter, but then Anice is so very pretty and the Airl, like most men in Cartreff, seems to value that above all other things.

Reeve, however, seems to have listened to Lady Rhoswen. He may not be able to herd goats, but when it comes to people, he is not useless.

In fact, he may be useful. But to be useful, I have to trust him.

Can I trust him?

"Well?" he asks, and I drag my unruly thoughts back to the matter at hand. "What's it to be? Are you going to let me help you? Are we going to help each other? As it stands, you're currently heading to a nunnery and I'm going to be packed off to die at sea, so . . ."

Despite momentary confusion at the "die at sea" comment, and with a small prayer to Lady Cassandra to forgive me, I decide to tell him . . . some of it. Because the fact of the matter is that my lady and I are in deep, deep trouble, and it will take someone with a lot to lose to help us.

But I cannot look at him, so I focus on a point just above his shoulder, gazing up the hill over the empty road to the castle gates. It is so quiet here that I fancy I can hear squirrels gnawing nuts in the forest. Or perhaps that is just the churning inside me.

"He —" I break off, squinting a little. No, it is not my imagination, although it is not the sound of squirrels — the gates are creaking slowly open.

"He?" prompts Reeve.

"Sorry," I say, shifting my gaze from the gates to his face. "There's no time now, we have to hide."

"Hide?" Reeve repeats, turning to look behind him. "Why should we hide?"

I exhale sharply, itching to be away. "Because here we are, two people new to Rennart Castle, with no real allies within its walls, standing on the roadside beside a body."

Reeve blanches, his face almost the same color as his clotted cream hair. "But all we did was find him," he stutters. "We didn't hurt him."

"No," I say, grabbing his hand and dragging him back across to the wooded side of the road. "We didn't, but have you not learned your lesson? Are you not content with simply being accused of stealing the Fire Star? Do you want to add this to your list of problems as well? To them, we are outsiders, Reeve, and nobody is more vulnerable than a person who is *other*." I tug once again at his hand.

Reeve says nothing but finally catches my worry, and allows himself to be led into the maze of trees. I can almost hear the thoughts grinding in his head as he stumbles along behind.

"Where are you taking me?" he asks, as I drag him deeper into the woods, as fast as I can make him go. Here, in the dim coolness of the trees, our footsteps are almost silent, muffled by generations of leaf litter, but I fancy that those traveling on the road behind us will be able to hear us breathe if they choose to listen.

Moments later, however, comes the dull, rhythmic thud of horse hooves moving at speed — too fast to see a body in the brambles on the side of the road, I hope. Trembling, I hear the sound come closer, closer, closer, before beginning to fade away.

"Keep walking," I whisper to Reeve, ignoring his question.

"But they've gone past us!" he protests in an overly loud voice. "We should head back to the castle so I can tell Sir Garrick about the sweeping man . . . Unless there is some reason you do not wish me to do that."

I lift my skirts a little to clear a boggy patch of the forest floor, grateful for my foresight in slipping out of the dainty soft-soled slippers that fashionable ladies — and their companions — must wear indoors and into the pair of sturdy lace-up boots I'd found by the kitchen door.

"I need to talk to someone," I demur. "And I know that you would not wish a young lady to be left to wander the forest alone."

I look sideways just in time to catch the suspicious glance Reeve throws my way. But, as I knew they would, his innate good manners and chivalry win out. "Indeed, my lady," he responds smoothly after a moment. "I would not wish such a thing. Particularly for one so unworldly and demure as yourself."

I suppress a grin. Two can play at this game.

"Oh, good Sir Almost Knight, what a brave and kind gentleman you are. I will not miss the opportunity to sing of your courtliness to Sir Garrick and my Lady Cassandra."

There is a pause. "I thought we'd agreed not to do this," Reeve says before muttering a sharp "ouch." His gait hitches, and it seems he is still wearing his house boots, and that the leaf litter may not be as soft as I'd thought.

"Why can't you just tell me where we're going?" he protests.

I stop and turn to face him, dropping his hand, which I had not even realized I was still holding.

"I cannot," I say. "I should not even be taking you with me. But it seems I find myself in the awkward position of needing you, Reeve of Norwood."

He studies my face for a moment, and I have the uncomfortable feeling that he is staring into my very thoughts. "Er, thank you," he says. "I think. So I should just . . . follow?"

I want to laugh at the expression on Reeve's face, but I say nothing, leaving him to work through his thoughts.

When you've been raised as this boy has been raised, the idea of following a girl anywhere goes against everything you know.

"All right," he says, and I blink at the rapid acquiescence. "But you owe me an explanation."

I hide my surprise and rapidly recalculate my opinion of him yet again as we continue, weaving our way through the trees. I had not thought he would agree so readily. It seems that the Lady Rhoswen has indeed done more than teach him a serving fork from an eating awl – or that "die at sea" comment was less of an exaggeration than I'd imagined.

Still, I can't help but wonder how he will react when I remove my sock in a few minutes to blindfold him.

CHAPTER ELEVEN

"You want to what?"

Reeve shook his head, as though to unscramble her words. He'd had just about enough of traipsing about in the forest with this strange, bossy girl. He could feel the beginnings of a large, watery blister on the ball of his foot and didn't dare to look at the soles of his boots to see just what a mess they were.

He had been about to turn around and return to Rennart Castle to change into more suitable footwear, cursing his lack of forethought, when he'd caught that flash of crimson in the brambles. Reeve was only pleased that he hadn't fainted when he'd realized it was blood — though he had to admit it had been a close call.

And now this.

"You have to wear this," Maven said, brandishing her sock at him even as she replaced the boot on her now-bare foot. "I can't take you any further if I don't cover your eyes."

"Don't be ridiculous," Reeve snapped. "I couldn't find my way back here if there was a knighthood wrapped in gold at the end of the trail. How can it possibly make any difference now?"

Maven said nothing, continuing to proffer the sock.

"No," Reeve repeated through gritted teeth. "I. Will. Not. Wear. The. Blindfold."

"Reeve," she said, her tone measured. "It is essential that I go . . . where I'm going. Now, I can either spin you around three times and push you off into the forest on your own to get lost, or, if you want those answers, you can put this over your eyes for about five minutes and we'll be there."

"Where is 'there'?" he demanded, before realizing there was a more pressing question. "And how do you even know where 'there' is? You're not from here, either!"

Maven blinked, and, at first, he thought she wasn't going to respond. "I've been before," she admitted.

Reeve thought about this. "You arrived last night," he said, talking out loud to himself. "But I saw you on the road much earlier. You came – 'there' – before you went to the castle."

He stopped, suddenly remembering the conversation the Airl and Sir Garrick had been having at dinner. The talk of treason, and uprising, of the King's spies . . .

"Are you a spy for the King?" Reeve blurted, wishing he could take back the words as soon as he'd spoken them. He had no weapon, and where there was one spy there were bound to be more. If she'd heard any rumors at all about the Airl's plans, then it was up to Reeve to stop her right now, before she had the chance to destroy them all!

"What?" It was Maven's turn to look astounded. "No! One thousand times no. I wouldn't spy for that bounder if you paid me. Which I suppose he would, given the way he's spending."

"I don't think you're supposed to say that out loud," Reeve muttered, peering into the trees around them to make sure they were quite alone.

"What? Bounder?" Maven repeated, and Reeve could see her trembling. "You would prefer that I call him a villain? That's what he is. My father gambled away our entire family fortune in the company of that wastrel when he was Prince. Now, he's King, and sitting on a golden throne, dressed in the finest silks, and building three new palaces he does not need, while my father drinks away what little money he has left!"

The last words were a shout that echoed through the trees, setting a nearby bird to flight, and Maven paused before going on in a fierce whisper. "I have no ties to him. Why would you ask me a question like that? What do you know?"

"I, er, well, I know nothing," Reeve said, quailing before her cold, curious stare. There was no way he was going to provoke her further or repeat to this puzzling girl what he'd overheard at the table. Not when he was already dealing with a dead man on the road, a missing jewel, an angry Airl and a reluctant bride. "Here, give me that sock. I will wear your blindfold."

Anything to change the subject.

With a searching look, Maven gave him the sock, saying nothing as he tied the soft fabric over his eyes. To his surprise, the sock smelled faintly of lavender and rose water, a distinctly different odor to that of his own socks. What's more, with his eyes covered, Reeve noticed that he could hear the birdsong more clearly – not to mention a skittering sound in the leaf litter to his left. The slight breeze ruffled his hair.

"Maven?" he asked, annoyed to hear a faint wobble in his voice. What was it about covering your eyes that made the whole world unfamiliar?

"Here," she said, and now her voice was gentle as she took his hand. "Don't worry, it's not far and I won't let you fall."

Despite Maven's words, Reeve stumbled as she led him forward.

"Stay close," Maven warned, pulling him toward her, so close that he could feel her skirts brush against his boots. "The ground is uneven."

Reeve exhaled sharply, hating how defenseless he felt as he crept along behind her, wondering just what it was that he was getting himself into. Maven's outburst had shocked him — not just her words, but the intense feeling that had forced them from her, when Reeve had thought her so contained, so sure of herself, so . . . cold. He was torn between feeling sorry for her and being very worried that all of that anger he'd just glimpsed might have led her to take drastic action.

She might not be a spy for the King, but Maven was into something up to her neck, and Reeve's very presence here was making him complicit.

Reeve pushed the thought away. The Airl had charged him with finding the Fire Star, and Reeve's very future as a knight depended on that. A knight would not run away, not when his gut told him that he was on the right track — even if that track did require him to blunder about wearing a blindfold.

"It's not far now," Maven said, breaking into his thoughts. "About twenty more steps."

Reeve concentrated on counting the steps.

"Okay," she said, dropping his hand as he felt the sun burning on his face. They had left the shadowy twilight of the forest and stepped into a clearing of some sort. He reached up to remove the blindfold.

"Not just yet," Maven said, putting her hand on his to still the fingers that were already working at the knot. "Wait here."

Reeve heard her walk away and then, inexplicably, the creaking sound of a door opening. Within moments, she was back, grabbing his hand again. "Follow me," she said, "but be prepared for steps. I'll tell you when."

"Maven —" he began, as she dragged him forward.

"I'll answer all your questions in a minute," she said, cutting off his protest. "But now, put one hand on my shoulder and step when I tell you to."

"Is all this entirely necessary?" Reeve asked, even as he allowed her to place his hand on her shoulder. "Really?"

"Really," Maven confirmed. "You'll see. Now, step."

Reeve did as he was told, nearly falling on his face as his foot dropped, his other hand clawing for Maven's other shoulder. "Steady!" she yelped, and he realized he was digging his fingers into her skin.

"You could have warned me that it was a long way down," Reeve grumbled.

"Oh, stop being a baby," she said. "You didn't fall, did

129

you? Now, step again – this one is smaller."

So the stairs were not even? Where was she taking him?

"Come on, Reeve," Maven encouraged. "Only a few more."

He said nothing, simply stepping when she told him to do so, his mind churning with questions.

At last, Reeve arrived on what felt like solid ground. To his surprise, he could feel the chill of cobblestones under the thin soles of his boots.

"All right," Reeve said, reaching for the blindfold. "I'm taking this off now."

Maven said nothing, and this time he didn't bother with the knot, pulling the sock from his eyes in one movement.

For a moment, Reeve thought he'd somehow damaged his sight forever but, gradually, his eyes began to adjust to the gloom, and he realized that he was standing in some kind of room. The room had no windows, and the only sources of light were from a faint glow from above him, at the top of the winding stairs he'd just come down, and a warm red from the dying coals in the huge stone fireplace that took up most of the wall beside him.

Maven was standing beside a long, wooden table, and, as he watched, she took a thin taper from a box on a shelf that was carved into the sandstone wall, and pushed it into the coals until it took light. She then used it to light the candles on three tall candelabra down the middle of the table, and the room was revealed.

Reeve stared open-mouthed as the scale of the space became clear.

"What is this place?" he blurted, his voice seeming to disappear into the stone walls. The ceiling was high and vaulted, carved into a dome that sat above the long table. Intricate carvings of birds and leaves, flowers and bees, suns and moons, stars and fantastic winged creatures adorned every tiny inch of the ceiling, as well as an arch that led into darkness at the far end of the room. Above the arch, inset as a circular coat of arms would be, was the same trees-and-bird symbol that Reeve had noticed on the muslin that wrapped the Lady Cassandra's wedding gown, and he frowned before turning his gaze to the rest of the room.

An enormous carved wooden chest sat to one side of the arch, the only furniture in the room besides the table and chairs. Above it hung a huge gilt-framed mirror, its unpolished frame reflecting dull gold in the candlelight. Reeve caught sight of his own face, pale and distorted, reflected in its cloudy surface, as Maven took the stairs two at a time and closed the door above them with a bang.

"It's a meeting room," said Maven, answering his question as she made her way back down the stairs.

"Take a seat. She'll be here soon."

As Maven spoke, she took her sock from his hand and, pulling out the nearest chair with an unceremonious scrape along the stone floor, dropped heavily into it and began tugging at her boot.

Reeve shook his head, the strangeness of the room creating an agony of nerves within him. "No," he said firmly. "I have done all you asked without question, but now you must answer. I'll not stay here a moment longer without that."

"I know you're curious," Maven said wearily, slipping the sock over her toes. "You would not have come this far without that. Can you really not wait another few minutes?"

But Reeve had had enough, and the calm way in which she performed the everyday task of putting her boot back on annoyed him. "No," he repeated. "You have made me complicit in whatever mess you're involved in, and I have a right to know what that is."

To his surprise, Maven laughed. "I have made you complicit," she said and groaned. "Reeve, have you not yet realized that you and I 'make' nothing? Your Sir Garrick will decide for you, just as the Lady Cassandra decides for me. The only choices we have are what we do with those decisions. Can we make them work and therefore save ourselves? Or will we be dragged to rack and ruin under their loving care?"

Reeve felt his brow furrow at her words, even as he caught sight of his own confused-looking reflection in the mirror. He didn't even look like himself down here, he realized, his usually bright golden hair dulled to a mousy brown by the light and the mirror's distorted surface.

"They do what they think is best," Reeve said, but even he could hear the doubt in his voice. Were they talking about the Lady Rhoswen, there would be no hesitation in his words. He had always trusted her implicitly, even when he was champing at the bit to be promoted from page to squire and she had made him wait, and wait, determined that Sir Garrick was the only knight sponsor for him.

But now? Could Reeve honestly say that Sir Garrick knew what was best for him? The Knight Protector barely knew Reeve – if anything, he seemed to swing from tolerating his presence to thinking Reeve useless.

"Reeve," Maven said, and now her voice was sad. "They do what they think is best for them. Never forget that."

Reeve found he needed to sit down, all thoughts of escaping up the staircase to the fresh air halted by the reality of his situation. The truth was that the Airl was ready to throw him from the castle in the next day or so, with no home and no future prospects, based simply on the fact that he needed a scapegoat for a burglary that should never have happened under the Airl's own roof.

And now the man that Reeve had thought might know something, his only lead for information, was lying dead in a ditch by the side of the road. Alone and unlamented by anyone bar he and Maven – and even they had left him to lie there.

"Tell me," Reeve said, his rising anxiety squeezing his voice to a higher pitch. He cleared his throat and took a deep breath. He may not feel like himself in this room, or even look like himself, but he would sound like himself if it took every ounce of poise and self-control the Lady Rhoswen had instilled in him.

"Tell me," Reeve repeated, and this time there was no tremble or squeak.

CHAPTER TWELVE

I have put it off as long as I can. Now that I have brought us both to safety, away from any prying eyes and eager ears that may be loitering, I can avoid this no longer. Simply by bringing Reeve to our sanctuary, I have enmeshed him in my plans, and I must hope that he has enough to lose not to bring me undone.

Reeve sits quietly enough, the candlelight bringing a dull glow to his fair hair, but his tension is evident in the way his fists lie clenched upon the table.

He will not move until he knows.

"His name was Sullivan and he had the Fire Star," I say on a sigh, gesturing in the general direction of the body in the brambles. Reeve says nothing, waiting for me to go on.

"You were right to suspect him," I continue, evoking a small half smile from Reeve — a smile that I know will disappear at my next words. "My Lady Cassandra dropped the stone to him this morning moments before she screamed."

Reeve blanched and then nodded. "I had wondered . . . But I couldn't quite believe. Then again . . . the perfect cover. Everyone in the courtyard was looking up at her as he made off with the stone. But who is he? A man that could be trusted with such a task."

I think carefully about my next words. "A loyal servant," I say, as my tears begin to fall and I dash them away with the back of my hand. "A man who would follow his mistress to the ends of the earth."

"Poor soul," Reeve says, crossing himself. "He did not deserve this."

"No," I say fiercely, wiping my tears away. "He did not."

Reeve is still working through my story. "But how?" he asks. "He did not travel with you. I saw you on the road, and there were but the two of you."

I say nothing, and he sits back in his chair, giving me a long, assessing look.

"This was not spur-of-the-moment," Reeve says, and now perplexed wrinkles mark his forehead. "He came ahead of you . . . he got himself a job . . ."

Reeve is shaking his head. "What did you do?" he asks, and even though he does not seem to expect an answer, I give him one.

"I did as my lady asked me to do," I say, mustering up as much dignity as I can manage when I feel so sick and tired. "I tried to find her a way out."

"But why you?" he asks, his confusion obvious. "Why in the name of all things sacred would she choose a servant girl to organize her life for her?"

"Companion," I correct through clenched teeth.

Reeve pushes his chair back and jumps to his feet. "Words," he says, pointing to my plain brown dress as he paces past. "You said yourself that you dress like a servant so as not to forget your place. And yet you tell me now that you are organizing your mistress's life just so. Even Lady Cassandra describes you as having many talents . . ."

Reeve stops pacing and turns to face me once more. "Just what are those talents, Maven? What am I missing here?"

I try to laugh it off with a toss of my hair and a flirtatious smile. "Why, just look at me?" I simper. "Can you not see? Are my talents not obvious?"

"Don't be ridiculous!" Reeve snaps, and, despite everything, I feel a pang. I do not need this pretty boy's approval, but his curt dismissal hurts me in a way I thought I'd grown beyond.

"Sorry," Reeve says, and I rearrange my expression, which must have given away my inner turmoil. "I did not mean to offend – I just meant that we have already agreed to do away with all that . . . stuff!" He waves a hand between us, and I remember our deal to avoid courtly banter. "That's all."

Somewhat mollified, I stand to face him. Over his shoulder, I can see my face like an apparition in the old mirror on the wall, pale and waxy and . . . unremarkable.

"It's okay," I say. "I understand."

Reeve says nothing, still waiting for me to explain. I turn from him with a sigh, wondering just how much to tell him. How much can I trust this boy who stands out in a crowd as much as I blend in?

"You might as well tell me," he says, as though reading my very thoughts. "What could possibly be worse than putting in motion a plan to steal a stone worth a king's ransom and getting a man killed in the process? Hmmm? What?"

He is right. He already knows too much about me. All I can do is give him the whole of it and then do something that I thought I would never do again. Hope.

"I can read," I whisper, feeling as though the words are being pulled from within me by force, and I hear his sharp intake of breath. "I can write. I can name every star in the night sky, I can make you a poultice, I can argue politics, I can discuss science, I can play chess."

Even as I make the admission, I wonder if I have read him correctly. Will he repay my trust, my hope, and keep my secrets? For if he does not, I will not be able to run far enough, fast enough, to survive.

"Are you a witch?" Reeve's voice squeaks on the last word. "Like Lady Cedwyn of Lygon?" He steps back and instinctively reaches for his belt, where his sword would hang if he were wearing one.

What can I do but laugh? Just last year, poor Lady Cedwyn had been discovered in her father's study, teaching herself the basics of physicking from an old book on the shelf. A book her father had probably never read, having "acquired" it after a nearby abbey had all but burned to the ground.

Perhaps it was a Beech Circle member who had taught Cedwyn her letters, I do not know, but, in Cartreff, where women are deemed "inferior learners" and therefore not worth teaching, her ability to read was taken as a sign that dark forces were at work. I do not blame Reeve for his reaction, but I am tired of living in a place where my cleverness is a liability.

"You have nothing to fear from me," I say. "I am no witch. There is no magic here, no spell, no potion. I do not even believe such things exist. I am just . . . lucky. And cursed."

Reeve pales at the word, and I kick myself for using it out loud. "Not cursed like that," I say, feeling the urgency rise within me. I must make him understand, and quickly.

"It's just an expression. I mean, I was lucky enough to have a father who recognized in me a mind that would be forever questing, fortunate that he was not frightened of a girl like me, and . . . cursed that he could not beat his own demons, meaning I have been consigned forever to my own nightmare."

I cannot even look at Reeve, but it matters not. The weight of his stare hangs upon me.

"He educated you? Your own father?" he asks, horrified. "Even knowing the consequences for you – and for him – were it to be discovered that you were educated? That you know and understand things that women and girls cannot know?"

The consequences. That I would be considered "unearthly" and burned as a witch, my father forced to watch in silence, carrying the burden of guilt and grief the rest of his days.

"I confess that I have spent many long nights wondering if it was that very fact that sent him to the pleasure parlors and gaming tables in the first place," I say. "He knew he was risking my life, but could not help himself, and I was ever thirsty to know more. Perhaps he lived with that risk through the thrill of gambling."

I will not admit that this is the opinion that my

mother and sisters have taken, and the reason they will never speak to me again. They won't tell anyone about me, about what my father did — they cannot, without condemning themselves as well — but they choose to keep me at a distance. The greater the distance the better, as far as they're concerned and, to be honest, as far as I'm concerned, too.

It is not easy to live with the idea that your own family is frightened of you.

Reeve pauses, and I find myself wiping my damp palms on my skirt before shoving them in my pockets. My fingers curl reassuringly around my silent, waiting knife, a steadying weight.

"Now I understand your anger at your father," Reeve says. "And at Lorimer."

I look up, startled.

"Oh, don't act so surprised," he says. "I'm good at two things, Maven — observation and people. You were seething in Lorimer's company, despite your best efforts to remain polite."

I let go of my knife and bring my hands back into the open. "He could have done more to help my father," I say. "To stop my father. He was the Steward of the Household — he knew when things started to become dire, when the silver plates began disappearing to pay debts, and yet he said nothing to my mother, or to anyone. Instead, he helped my father into further debt to keep him afloat, in the Prince's company, at the gaming tables, while Lorimer secured himself another position. Then, Lorimer left, while we picked up what few pieces were left."

Reeve begins to pace again. "Does he know? Lorimer, I mean, does he know about you?"

"Nobody outside the immediate family knows. My father was careful about that. He is good at keeping secrets when he wants to be."

Reeve nods. "But the Lady Cassandra knows," he states, looking at me in the mirror even as his back is to me. "About you, I mean."

Again, I find myself wondering just how much I dare tell him.

"Some," I settle for.

Cassandra knows I can read and write, because one day she caught me in her father's library. She keeps my secret because it has proven useful to her, over and over again. It is why we are able to smirk together over "sorcery" and "pitiless bad luck."

She does not know, however, the extent to which my father taught me about the art of war and strategy during long nights over a chessboard, and with maps and bronze armies on paper battlegrounds.

She does not know how he schooled me in the inner workings of the King's court, that he could see the disastrous present of our "noble" King laid out like a path from the Prince's earliest days as an indulged child in the palace gardens.

She does not know that my father would come home in the early hours and wake me, a child of nine or ten, to fill my ears with drunken stories of the hustling and maneuvering of the men who ebbed and flowed around the then heir to the throne, trying to parlay friendship into power.

The Lady Cassandra does not need to know these things.

Not yet.

Reeve settles another long look upon me.

"Maven," he says quietly, but I can feel the tension in him. "Where is the Fire Star?"

Turning to him, I take a deep breath and give him my first truly honest answer since we met.

"I don't know," I admit, fighting the panic rising within me — the panic I've been distracting myself from ever since I clapped eyes on the body in the brambles. "Reeve, I don't know."

He stares at me. "What do you mean, you don't know?"

Reeve couldn't believe what he was hearing. That Maven and Lady Cassandra had set up the entire disappearance of the Fire Star in the first place was bad enough. That the conduit for the deceit was now dead in a ditch and Maven had no idea where the stone was – well, that was quite another thing.

"He had it," Maven whispered through thin, pale lips as though the dire reality of the situation had only just dawned on her. "Sullivan had it. And now it is not there."

Reeve sank into a chair. If the sweeping man – Sullivan – had taken the Fire Star beyond the castle walls, then right now the stone could be . . . anywhere. He groaned.

"You were out here to meet him," Reeve said, turning to Maven. "That's why you followed me, why you 'happened' along the road when you did. Were you to meet this Sullivan here?" He waved a hand in the air above his head, taking in the quiet room around them.

"Not here," Maven said, dropping onto a straight-backed wooden chair across from him. "That would never do. I was to meet him at the bottom of the hill, take back the Fire Star and bring it here. But –"

She didn't need to go on.

"So Sullivan definitely had it on him," Reeve groaned again. "It left the castle walls."

"I can only assume he would not have come to the meeting place without it," she whispered.

Reeve exhaled. "So it's gone. Thanks to you and Lady Cassandra, the Airl's precious family heirloom, worth a fortune, is . . . gone. And with it my future!"

144

"My future, too," Maven reminded him, her voice barely audible as she studied the worn wooden tabletop. "I didn't know this would happen, Reeve. I thought the plan was foolproof. We told no one . . ."

Reeve thumped the table in frustration, and Maven jumped. "No plan is foolproof," he said. "And somebody knew."

He paused to let that sink in before going on. "We need to get it back – for both our sakes. You need to think about who else could have known about this little plan of yours."

"No one," she snapped, her open-palmed slap on the table echoing his own. "Myself, the Lady Cassandra and Sullivan. That's it. And do not thump the table at me, Reeve of Norwood."

Taken aback by her vehemence, Reeve bowed and forced himself to relax. "My apologies, Maven of Aramoor. I am . . . overwrought."

He sat back, considering Maven's words – and all he now knew of the Fire Star's disappearance, and those who were involved. "Did Sullivan provide the boot print in Lady Cassandra's room?" he asked.

"His boot did," Maven admitted. "I collected it from him after everyone had gone to bed, and returned it a short while later."

"And did anyone see you wandering the halls of Rennart Castle with a man's boot under your arm?"

Reeve asked, unable to control the sarcasm in his voice.

"No," she said, as though it was a silly question. "Though I saw others wandering. You, for starters."

"I was not wandering," he said, sitting up straight. "I put Sir Garrick to bed and returned to my own room. I saw no one else —" Reeve broke off, as a memory suddenly surfaced.

"Did you see someone run into me?" he asked. In the upheaval of his day, he'd all but forgotten being bowled over in the dark.

Maven pushed her chair back, wincing as it scraped across the cobblestones. "I caught a glimpse," she said. "It was not long after I'd left my lady's rooms."

"Did you know him?"

"I had seen him before. He was in a group of men ordered from the Great Hall just before Lady Cassandra announced herself."

Reeve froze. "What did he look like?" he asked, putting aside the fact that Maven had even been present for that moment in the Hall. He had not seen her, but then who would have done so when all attention was fixed on her mistress?

"Scruffy," she said. "Dark hair. Unshaven. Staggering."

Reeve just managed to stop himself from thumping the table again. "Brantley! It had to be him. But why was he running through the halls after dark?"

And courting the Lady Anice in the garden the very

next day, Reeve finished silently. That was a piece of information he was keeping to himself for the time being. The fewer people who knew of the liaison, the better for Lady Anice's good name.

"You think Brantley had something to do with all this?" Maven didn't look convinced. "I'd never seen him before that night. I can't see how he would know anything about the Fire Star."

Reeve had to agree with her, but he also knew from his experience of completing colorful picture puzzles with Lady Rhoswen that every piece had a place. Some seemed as though they would never fit anywhere until, all of a sudden, they were the perfect shape to slip into a space.

Brantley was disgruntled and unhappy. Quite what Lady Anice saw in him, Reeve couldn't say, but Brantley's discontent made the man dangerous in any court.

"I don't know what he knows," Reeve said out loud to Maven. "But we need to find out. Everyone in the castle is a suspect, until they're not."

Maven raised one eyebrow. "How do you know that poor Sullivan wasn't set upon randomly by thieves?"

Reeve paused. "I don't," he admitted.

"Well, I do," Maven said, jumping to her feet. "There was no scuffle. If Sully had come across strangers, he would have run, or fought, hard. But there was no disturbance on the road at all, suggesting to me that he was happy enough to encounter his killer – or, at least, had to be civil."

Reeve did not miss the growing excitement in Maven's voice as she continued: "And, given he'd been in the castle only a few days, that narrows the field."

"I wish that were the case," Reeve said, not wanting to dampen her enthusiasm. He realized that, even though their situation was dire, a small part of Maven was enjoying the chance to use what Reeve was beginning to suspect was a formidable mind.

"He was working as a groundskeeper, Maven, sweeping every corner of the great courtyard every day. Over the course of just a few days, he would have seen every knight, squire and servant in the castle. Gads, he probably even knew where that shirker Neale is hiding! Sullivan may not have known the name of his killer, but he would have recognized any person from Rennart Castle – even if they weren't wearing livery."

Maven bit her lip and groaned. "You're right," she said, slumping back into the chair opposite him once more. "So we have no leads."

They sat in perplexed silence for a moment, allowing Reeve to gather his thoughts – and realize that, on a day of many questions, he still didn't have an answer to the one that had seemed most urgent not that long ago.

"Maven," he said. "Where are we? And who are we waiting for?"

CHAPTER THIRTEEN

I open my mouth to speak but, before I can get a word out, there's a creak from the top of the stairs, followed by a brief flash of light and the sound of the wooden door being pulled closed.

"You'll see," I murmur to Reeve, who says nothing but turns to face the stairs.

There is a soft swish of skirts on the steps and then a pair of sturdy boots, worn as lightly as dancing slippers, appears.

"Ah, Maven," says Myra, her smooth, silvery voice like music to my ears. I met this woman only one day ago, but she emanates a soothing calm that is both rare and instantly trustworthy – even for me. It's also totally at odds with her outer appearance, I acknowledge, taking in her wild curls and ragged, patched gown.

"And you, young sire?" Myra continues, her glance skipping over Reeve's face before landing on my own, the questions obvious in her startling green eyes. "It is a long time since one such as you has graced this room."

I bow my head, knowing that I have stretched a very new friendship by bringing Reeve here. "I had no choice but to bring him," I say. "I was worried for his safety."

"My safety? What are you talking about? And how do you two know each other?" Reeve sounds torn between outrage and bewilderment, but I say nothing until Myra indicates with a small smile that I should answer.

I open my mouth, then close it again, worried about how much to reveal. How much more to reveal. Myra seems to sense my hesitation.

"I think we can trust the young squire with our secret," she says to me. "After all, he has trusted me with one of his."

Reeve blanches, and even I can hear the underlying tenor of threat in Myra's statement. What does she know of him, and why would he be so worried about it? I file the questions away for later, but ask them I will. I have given Reeve my secrets, and I will be safer if I hold his in return. But for now it is enough that Myra knows them.

"I'll begin with your question about safety," I say, getting to my feet and walking alongside the length of the table as I speak. "You found a dead man on the road, Reeve, and without thought or caution hurried toward him. What if the killer was still there, hidden in the bushes beside the body?"

I turn in time to catch him flinch. "Or what if," I continue, strolling as casually as I can back toward him, "it had not been me who found you, but another, less trusting, person who decided that *you* were the killer? Had you considered that? What defense would you have given?"

Myra's face is impassive, but Reeve's mouth has tightened into a grim line as he considers the implications of my narrative.

"The Airl and Sir Garrick charged me with finding the Fire Star," he says, sounding stubborn. "I would have explained that I was carrying out my duties."

"And as I explained to you on our way here, you have no allies in that castle, Reeve. Not yet. You are dispensable, and they have no reason to trust that you did not kill Sullivan yourself and pocket the stone. At the very least, they would carry out their threat to send you back home to your father, your dreams of a knighthood up in smoke."

As Reeve flinches at my words, I can see Myra's lips purse as she takes in the full picture of his situation, filing it away. Members of the Beech Circle well know the power of observation and information.

"So, I brought you here to hide you while we considered our next moves," I continue, "and waited to speak to one who knows this area, and its people, very well."

Myra acknowledges my words with a tilt of her chin.

"But you haven't explained how you even knew this place was here, or how you know Myra, despite arriving at Rennart Castle so recently," Reeve says. Despite his still-polite demeanor, his growing impatience is unmasked by the rapid beat he is tapping out with his forefinger on the table.

I sigh, seeking Myra's reassurance before I continue. It goes against the edicts of our Circle to tell him more, but Myra nods again.

"I told you this is a meeting place," I begin, and now I come to sit back down in my chair opposite Reeve. It is imperative that he understand the seriousness of what I am about to say.

"There is a . . . group of girls and women," I continue, ignoring the wrinkle that appears between his brows at my words and forging ahead. "We do not all know each other but we are . . . connected."

The wrinkle deepens. "Connected?" Reeve echoes.

"We look out for each other," Myra says, and I sit back, relieved that I will not have to explain it all. For how can

I possibly sum up the Beech Circle?

"We look for ways to help each other," Myra goes on.

Reeve sits back in his seat. "Ways to help each other what?"

"Escape," I answer. "Become something other than a possession to be traded to the highest bidder in marriage."

Reeve blinks. "You would run from everything you know?"

"As far and as fast as I can," I confirm. "But where can I go? Without family blessing I have no money, without money I have no choices. A girl in Cartreff today is at the mercy of the fates, and the fates are decided by those around her."

Reeve thinks a moment. "You don't live like that," he says, turning to Myra. "From what I have heard, you live as you please."

Myra smiles gently at him. "That's because it pleases me to live simply, on the edge of the forest owned by the Airl, surrounded by nature. They leave me alone, for now, because I have the skills to help them birth their children and mend their broken bones. But I also know that my very precarious existence is at the whim of the Airl, and that he can end my freedom at any time. It is not a life many are born to, or would choose."

Reeve says nothing, seeming to digest her words.

"But you are not witches?" he asks, uneasily.

Myra laughs, and I join in. "No," she says. "Not unless witches are just women who choose to ask questions."

I can see him trying to process all we are telling him, and Myra, too, senses his discomfort. "Would it help you to know that we count noblewomen among our number? A lady or two whose names you may know well," she says, her voice soft.

Reeve gasps and his eyebrows are nearly in his hairline, but he is not as surprised as I am. For Myra to share that information with Reeve, she must be very sure of his secret.

"What?" he all but shrieks. "No! Lady Rho—"

"No names," Myra interrupts.

"But I have seen no sign of any such thing," Reeve says, shaking his head. "My — one particular lady I have in mind is not book learned. The Airl, er, her husband would not stand for it."

Myra laughs again. "You will never see a sign unless you know what to look for. And some have arranged their lives in such a way that they are able to conduct it much as they wish. Not all are fortunate enough to have two separate residences and a husband who avoids country life."

Reeve looks pained at that specific detail. "I had never thought of it that way. When I thought about it at all, I assumed it was, er, her husband who liked his lady safe at . . . in the country."

Myra chortles. "And I think that the particular lady is very happy to have the world think that way."

But Reeve has other questions. "Are there other meeting places like this one? Near Harding, for instance?"

Myra shakes her head. "Not like this one," she says. "There are only four like this in the whole kingdom. But we do not need a room like this in which to meet."

"I don't understand how this works at all," Reeve says, raking his fingers through the blond stubble on his head. "How many of you are there?"

I wonder just how much Myra will tell him, and am unsurprised when she simply shakes her head again. "No, young sire," she says. "To know more puts us – and you – in great danger. Suffice that you understand that we are here to help Maven and Cassandra – and now you – in whatever way we can."

She turns to me. "I assume it has gone wrong?"

I quickly fill her in on the true disappearance of the Fire Star while Reeve watches on, arms folded across his chest.

Myra frowns as I speak, shaking her head sadly over Sullivan's death. "Someone has told," I say, winding down my story. "Someone must have heard of our plans."

Myra stares along the table and down into the deep, dark space beyond the arch. I know that the doorway leads to a warren of rooms carved out of the sandstone, some furnished with iron beds to house women and children looking for refuge, others stacked to the roof with stores.

The Beech Circle may not be known to Reeve, but it has existed for generations, providing secret care and community for girls and women in need.

"I don't know how," Myra says. "The only people here yesterday were you, Cassandra and I, and I can't imagine you two have spoken of your plans within the castle walls?"

I shake my head fervently.

"Then someone saw," Myra says, with a toss of that wild hair. "Someone must have seen the precise moment that Sullivan took possession of the stone and decided they wanted it for themselves."

Reeve makes a strange choking sound. "I was in the courtyard and I saw nothing," he says. "Everyone was looking up at the Lady Cassandra."

Myra turns to him. "I wasn't," she says, and he blushes, making me wonder all over again about this secret they share. "You think that everyone was because you were. But there were at least fifty people in that courtyard."

My heart sinks. "Fifty," I repeat. "Then how can we ever find out who took the Fire Star?"

"Not we," Myra says, smiling. "You and Reeve.

Together. I will tend to Sullivan. You two will go back to the castle and you will ask the questions, seek the answers and find the truth."

She places a steadying hand on each of our shoulders. "After all," Myra says. "You both have a lot to lose if that jewel does not turn up, do you not?"

Reeve and I look at each other. I wonder if he feels as reluctant as I do. I am used to working alone to solve my problems.

"Then the time to begin is now," says Myra, drawing us both to our feet and giving us a gentle push toward the stairs. "You can hide down here no longer."

I want to tell her that I'm not hiding, but the truth is that, from the moment I realized the Fire Star was not in Sullivan's pockets, all I wanted to do was to run and to keep running. But now I must go back to Lady Cassandra and tell her that the Fire Star has truly gone.

And with it, her last chance to escape her fate.

Reeve is also dragging his feet. I do not envy him having to face the Knight Protector and the Airl to tell them he has precisely nothing.

"Come on, you two," says Myra with another little push. "You can do this. If you need help or have news, send a message. Maven, you know how."

I nod, thinking of Polly, the tiny scullery maid who has big dreams of escaping her life of drudgery in which time is measured by the rumbling of other people's stomachs. Members of the Beech Circle stretch across all facets of Cartreff life, each with a role to play. Polly's regular visits to the wyld woman in the woods for herbs are the perfect cover to keep Myra abreast of castle news, without Myra having to be seen too often within its walls. The Airl is, to be fair, more tolerant than many in his position when it comes to a woman like Myra. Perhaps it is Lady Rhoswen who helps him to see that Myra's knowledge of plants and herbs is a help to the people of Rennart, not a threat to its ruler? But Myra is careful not to push that tolerance too far.

"Come on," I say to Reeve now with more certainty than I feel. "We can do this."

I head up toward the door, hearing him on the stairs behind me, the heavy sound of his boots a dull counterpoint to the rapid beating of my own heart.

"Ah, there you are," Lorimer said, striding into the kitchen where Reeve was hastily finishing a cup of mead. Reeve had been surprised to discover on his return to the castle that he'd been gone less than two hours, and had taken the opportunity to gulp down a late lunch before reporting to Sir Garrick.

It felt as though a lifetime had passed since he'd

innocently ventured through the gate in search of Myra, and Reeve needed time to consider exactly what form that report would take.

His head was whirling with information, but Reeve could share none of it with Sir Garrick, or the Airl. Maven may not have recognized Myra's threat to reveal Reeve's little problem for what it was, but Reeve had. If Reeve revealed either the truth about the Fire Star or a hint about their secret Circle, Myra would ensure Sir Garrick knew that his new squire couldn't stomach the sight of blood. And there would go Reeve's dreams of becoming a knight.

If, on the other hand, Reeve went back to Sir Garrick with no updates at all, his dreams of becoming a knight looked precarious anyway.

At this point, the only thing that Reeve knew for sure was that Maven was at the heart of all his troubles – had she and her mistress not cooked up a scheme to spirit away the Fire Star, Reeve wouldn't be in this mess at all. In fact, he'd have nothing more on his mind than the best way to charm Cook into cutting him another slice of ham.

Reeve pushed down the surge of anger that seemed to accompany even the faintest thought of Maven right now. Myra had made it quite clear that their problems were tied together, which meant they needed to work together – not that Maven seemed open to the idea. She had said little on their walk back to the castle, refusing to be drawn into revealing more about the secret club she was part of.

And Lady Rhoswen! Even now, Reeve shook his head at that particular revelation. How she had been involved in something like that all the time he'd served her, Reeve couldn't even begin to imagine.

Though no names had been mentioned, he'd been a bit surprised that Myra had even hinted at the lady's involvement – until he realized that there was no one he could tell. Who on earth would ever believe him, a lowly squire in danger of being ousted from Rennart Castle? Not Sir Garrick or the Airl, that's for sure.

But if there was even the slightest bit of truth in Lady Rhoswen's involvement, then Reeve wasn't going to be able to mention the Beech Circle to anyone, either. Exposing Maven and Myra might also harm his lady, and there was no way in the world Reeve would do that to the woman who had been so kind to him.

Reeve had been churning this over with his lunch – and wondering how members even recognized each other – when he'd been winkled out by Lorimer.

"You were under strict orders to see me at once when you returned," the older man said now as Reeve jumped to his feet.

"Oh, hush," said Cook, tapping her ladle on Reeve's shoulder. "Surely, even you remember what it was like to be sixteen? A stomach on legs, that's what they all are."

"I have always known my duty," Lorimer sneered, looking down his nose at her. "That's why I'm where I am today – and why this boy is likely to end up back under his mother's feet before too long."

Reeve tried not to flinch at Lorimer's threat. "Sorry," Reeve said, "I didn't think a minute or two would make any difference. And I'm yet to see Sir Garrick."

Lorimer's lip curled again. "Surely you understand that your responsibility is first to the Airl, then to your master, then to *me*, then to your stomach."

Lady Rhoswen had always told him that silence was often the best and most encompassing response, particularly when you know you're in the wrong. Silence could be taken any way by another party and meant you were never required to admit or deny guilt.

So Reeve held his tongue and, as he'd suspected, Lorimer took this for acquiescence and gave Cook a smug look. The truth was that as far as Reeve was concerned, his first and only responsibility in this household was to Sir Garrick, to whom he was now bound.

Sir Garrick answered to the Airl, Reeve answered to Sir Garrick.

Lorimer was just someone that Reeve would need to learn to manage while he was here at Rennart Castle. And, from what Maven had revealed about the man, he might take careful management.

"Now," Lorimer was saying, and the smugness had not left his face. "Sir Garrick is looking for you. It seems as though your, er, personal errand has extended beyond the bounds of what he thought was a suitable length of time. You're to report to him immediately."

Gulping, Reeve wiped his fingers and face on the napkin that the sympathetic Cook handed him.

"Follow me," said Lorimer, turning about-face and stalking from the kitchen. Reeve gulped again. He had only a few minutes to work out exactly what he was going to tell Sir Garrick — and what he wasn't.

So deep in his own thoughts, filled with underground rooms carved with trees and birds and leaves, was Reeve that he followed Lorimer through the winding halls without even realizing it.

"Look lively, boy," Lorimer said under his breath before knocking on the door of Sir Garrick's chamber.

Reeve breathed a sigh of relief — at least he hadn't been taken to the Airl's solar. He wasn't sure he'd bear up under the scrutiny of both men with the scanty tale he was about to tell.

"Come," said Sir Garrick, and Lorimer opened the door, all but shoving Reeve through it.

"Ah, there you are," said Sir Garrick. "That will be all,

Lorimer."

Reeve thought he noted a small moue of disappointment on Lorimer's stern face as he was dismissed. Reeve wasn't sorry that the steward wasn't going to be witness to what Reeve suspected would be a severe dressing down.

Sir Garrick waited until the door shut with a click before turning to Reeve.

"Where is Neale?" he asked. "What have you done with him?"

Reeve stared, his head spinning with the unexpected questions. "I don't know where he is. Why would I do anything with him?"

Sir Garrick caught and held his stare. "I know Rhoswen wanted the squire role for you two years ago. Did she fill your head with nonsense and jealousy?"

"What?" Reeve all but shouted. "No! She explained to me that the Airl had chosen Neale over me. I was disappointed but I knew that Lady Rhoswen would ensure my future — if not with you, then with someone else."

Sir Garrick looked at him a moment longer. "I believe you tell the truth," he said, scratching the dark bristle on his chin. "But that does not negate the fact that Neale is missing. I have not seen him today."

Reeve blinked. "He has been gone since last night.

He was not waiting in your chambers after dinner. It was I who readied you for bed."

"Inasmuch as I was in a fit state to be readied," Sir Garrick muttered with a hoarse laugh.

There was a pause, and Reeve wondered if he was supposed to say something.

"Gads, what a terrible day it has been," Sir Garrick said, before sinking onto the edge of his bed. The movement of the mattress dislodged a chessboard on the side table, and half the pieces rattled to the floor. "I knew that this marriage would not be easy, but . . . it has not even begun."

Reeve waited, but nothing more was forthcoming. "Sir Garrick," he ventured. "Where would Neale go?"

Sir Garrick reached down to pick up a pawn beside his boot, twirling the piece between restless fingers. "I don't know," he admitted. "He was unhappy at the prospect of sharing the squiring duties. His father is a friend of the Airl's and made that quite clear. But I don't think he would run . . ."

Reeve held his breath as Sir Garrick sprang to his feet, sending a bishop and a rook skittering across the floor. "The Fire Star," Sir Garrick breathed. "Perhaps . . . Oh no, surely not."

Reeve gulped. Sullivan had stolen the Fire Star at Lady Cassandra's request. Neale had had nothing to do with that, and, in fact, had been missing since before the Fire Star had vanished. So, technically, Neale had had nothing to do with the stone's fake disappearance.

But . . . could Reeve discount the fact that Neale might have been responsible for Sullivan's death and stolen the Fire Star for real?

"You have no thoughts on this?" Sir Garrick prompted. "What did you discover when you went to find your 'person who may have seen something'? Did they see something? Was it Neale? Do not protect him if you know the truth."

Reeve knew that silence was not the answer this time. "I do not know Neale," he said, choosing his words with care. "Why then would I protect him?"

Sir Garrick was not placated. "Some sense of misplaced loyalty to a fellow squire?"

"I know nothing of Neale's disappearance," Reeve said, happy to be able to state the truth on this point. "I was surprised that he was not here to receive you last night, and I am more surprised to hear that he is not here now."

"I believe you," Sir Garrick said, giving Reeve a long look. "But the fact remains that Neale is missing and so is the Fire Star. I need to tell the Airl."

Sir Garrick brushed his hands down his side, seeming to gather himself. "Do you have anything further to add regarding your inquiries?" he asked, and Reeve did not miss the note of hope in his voice.

Having to tell the Airl that Sir Garrick's own squire was missing and was therefore the number one suspect in the disappearance of the Airl's family heirloom was clearly not a task to relish.

"I –" Reeve began. The truth was, he had much to tell Sir Garrick and the Airl. So much that would quickly ensure Reeve's place at Rennart Castle. But to do that, he would need to expose Maven, Lady Cassandra – and Myra. And exposing Myra meant exposing Reeve's secret – at which point any surety about Reeve's future went up in a puff of smoke anyway.

"Well, boy?" Sir Garrick asked.

"I do not," Reeve said, looking at his boots. "I did not find the person I sought."

This was not strictly untrue – the sweeping man was unable to answer questions, and Myra was not the person Reeve had imagined her to be.

"Let's get it over with then," said Sir Garrick, gesturing toward the door. "I have an engagement for a stroll in the garden with the Lady Cassandra."

He sounded as though he was being sent to the gallows.

"I, er, you want me to come with you?" said Reeve. "To the Airl, I mean."

Sir Garrick smiled without humor. "Yes," he said. "And, as my only remaining squire, you will also accompany me to the garden. It should prove a punishing afternoon all round for both of us."

Reeve could only bow acquiescence and lead the way, holding the door for the knight, trying to ignore the rolling sensation behind his belt as he did so.

Perhaps Lorimer was right. He should have waited to eat.

CHAPTER FOURTEEN

"What about here? The roses make a nice backdrop, don't you think?"

I look at my Lady Cassandra, who is artfully arranging herself with her blood-red skirts spread across the gray stone bench, the rose garden in full multicolored bloom behind her.

Shaking my head, I turn to point at a low stone wall. "Over there," I say. "The dark-green hedge will provide a better counterpoint to your gown."

Sighing, she stands and moves to the new position, once again spreading her skirts around her. "Is this better?" Cassandra asks, trying for sarcasm but undermined by the edge of anxiety in her voice.

I move forward to tuck one recalcitrant curl back into place behind her ear. I always feel that her true nature is revealed in the thick luxuriance of her hair, which I must fight into submission every morning with a comb.

"Perfect. He cannot help but be bowled over by your beauty."

Cassandra bites her lip. "And bowled over he must be," she says. "Or I am off to the nunnery, and so are you."

The full horror of the loss of the Fire Star has dawned on her little by little. When I first shared the news, she was full of sorrow and rage at Sullivan's death. Then came the realization that, without the stone, she has no option but to marry Sir Garrick, lest she find herself a penniless old maid.

After that came the horror that Sir Garrick may no longer wish to marry her without the stone. After all, the entire marriage is predicated on the Airl's desire to bring the Fire Star within his house.

Without the Fire Star, Cassandra is merely the youngest daughter, past her prime, of a minor noble. She will end up back in her father's household, likely never to leave again, condemned to dance attendance on her sisters and their offspring.

It pains me to see her spirit brought so low.

It was easy to talk about preferring the nunnery when the plan had been to take the Fire Star and run, secure in the knowledge that, with it in hand, Cassandra had the means to do as she pleased. But now?

"The Beech Circle will see us right," I whisper to her, adjusting the neckline of her gown so that her creamy skin is offset perfectly. She wears a delicate silver locket around her neck, and I can barely look at it, knowing the gown was designed with the Fire Star in mind.

Cassandra, however, reaches up now to grasp the locket, as though gaining strength from it. Inside the circle of the locket, behind the expected miniature portrait of her parents, is a little painting of trees and a red bird. The Beech trees, a symbol of knowledge and wisdom; the robin, which makes its home in hidden places but can fly as it pleases. Roots and wings, all in a circle.

"I know," Cassandra whispers back, tears pooled on her lashes. "I am grateful that you took me to them, Maven, that we have them for support. But . . ."

"I'm so sorry, my lady," I say into the silence as her words trail away, the apology drawn unbidden from my lips. I feel so responsible that our plans are in tatters, although I have gone over it and over it in my mind and cannot see where we went wrong, or who could possibly have known.

Cassandra rests her hand on the side of my face. "It is not your fault," she says. "We gambled and we lost.

And it was still worth the risk to imagine the life of freedom we could have led."

I shake my head. "Can still lead," I say. "I have not given up, my lady. I will find that stone."

Cassandra removes her hand, and her gaze follows it to her lap. "The wedding is the day after tomorrow," she says. "Half the guests are already here. Presuming that the Airl does not order Sir Garrick to call it off, you have no time to find the Fire Star. And even if you did, our plans for escape are in tatters. We are trapped, one way or another."

I open my mouth to speak, but she stops me. "He is here."

I melt away behind a small grove of almond trees, noting as I do that the picture we have created is perfect. Cassandra sits straight backed on the wall, her red gown bright against the deep-green leaves, a haughty smile upon her beautiful face. She looks powerful and in control, the antithesis of how she feels, and I admire once again her ability to do what she must to make the best of any situation.

I was with her when she learned of the death of her elderly betrothed, and watched as her future went up in smoke. She had known that they wouldn't be married long due to his age, but she'd also known that, as a widow, she would have had the freedom she had long craved.

Marriage to a young, vital man meant a long life of servitude and obedience. Neither of these were traits for which Cassandra was renowned.

"How did she take the news?"

I jump at the voice, turning from the scene in front of me where Sir Garrick and Lady Cassandra are making awkward small talk about the weather, to face Reeve.

"Don't creep up on me like that!" I sound like an angry viper.

"I didn't creep," Reeve whispers, holding up his hands as though for protection. "You were so involved in spying on my master that you didn't hear me."

"I am not spying," I say. "I am doing my duty as a chaperone."

"Good," he says, stepping up beside me to also peer around the bush. "So am I."

We watch in silence for a while, before turning to each other with a grimace. "It's going well, then," Reeve says, his tone mocking.

"Your knight needs more lessons in charming a lady," I say, watching Sir Garrick pulling on his ear as he tries to think of what to say next.

"His reputation suggests that he understands courtly love very well," Reeve says, as though speaking to a small child.

I stare at him, taking in the words "courtly love."

"If he's over there comparing her face to a summer's day, we're all in big trouble."

"What do you mean?" he asks.

I sigh. "Cassandra cannot stand all that folderol any more than I can. It's one of the reasons it took her so long to accept a betrothal, and the reason we get on so well."

Reeve frowns before crossing his arms, appearing to be deep in thought.

"Are you willing to help me to get these two better acquainted?" he says after a moment. "After all, when they marry in a few days, we are going to be spending an awful lot of time with the two of them, and it will help us all if they are . . . warmer to each other."

I glance at the stiff couple on the wall. "And just how do you propose to do that?"

"You mentioned to me that you play chess," he says, and I scan the garden to make sure no one has heard before nodding, unwilling to affirm his statement out loud. "Does she?"

"I have been teaching her," I whisper, wondering where he's going with this. "She is a beginner but she has promise."

"Wait here," he says, and is gone before I can ask any further questions.

Minutes pass and, with each, the conversation between the lady and her knight sputters further into oblivion. I hold my breath as Cassandra stares unseeingly into the blue sky, while Sir Garrick gazes at a stone statue of a dragon, as though willing it to life.

"Okay, take this over to her," says Reeve, startling me once again. He hands me a wooden chessboard and a small leather pouch, which I assume holds the pieces.

"I can't do that!" I say. "Then he'll know that she can play. You know that chess is not considered a ladylike pastime. Would you ruin her?"

He proffers the board again, shaking the pouch at me. "They are from Sir Garrick's quarters."

"Be that as it may . . ." I take the pieces and the board from him and stand, weighing them in my hands.

"Could it be worse than it is now?" he asks, and there is no malice in the mild query.

"If he reports to the Airl that she knows this game, it could be," I say, cursing my agony of indecision.

"It will be up to her to decide whether to take them," Reeve says. "We are just giving her the tools to perhaps forge an understanding. From what you tell me of your lady, she would welcome a . . . challenge in her life."

"She has enough challenges," I say, but the acid has gone from my tone.

"A friend then," Reeve says, and this time he flashes that winning smile, the dimple peeking from his cheek. "We could all use more friends — even you, Maven of

Aramoor, though you do not make it easy. And Sir Garrick is a good man, albeit one not born to nobility."

Ignoring his crack about friendship, I tuck the heavy board under my arm and grasp the pouch more firmly. "I'll take it to her, but what she does is up to her."

Reeve says nothing as I step out from behind the shrub and make my way toward my lady.

"Maven? What do you need?" I do not miss the note of eagerness in Cassandra's voice. I think she hopes that I bring a message summonsing her away.

"I, well, I, er –" I cannot believe how tongue-tied I am. The truth is that I am worried that I may be bringing more trouble upon my lady's head.

"You have something for my lady?" It is Sir Garrick who speaks, and I turn to look at him, for the first time, in the face. For a moment, I am speechless – his rough features have a quiet strength while his dark-brown eyes are kind upon me.

"Well, I –" I can almost hear Reeve laughing at me from behind the shrub, so I gather my composure. "I had wondered, my lady, if you might have some use for this."

I hold out the chessboard and pieces, but Cassandra does not move to take them. "Where did you get these? What use could I make of such a thing?" My heart sinks as I register her fury.

After a moment, however, Sir Garrick reaches for the pouch, opens it and looks inside. "It is as I thought," he murmurs. "This is my chessboard and my pieces. Where did you get them?"

I am saved from answering by the appearance of Reeve. "It was I who gave them to her," he says, with a small bow.

"Why would you imagine that Sir Garrick would require such a thing in this time and place?" Lady Cassandra demands.

Sir Garrick looks from Reeve to me, thoughtfully. "It is almost as though you expect that the Lady Cassandra might be able to play," he says.

"Oh, what nons—" Cassandra begins, but Sir Garrick is still speaking.

"Which would, indeed, be a fine discovery."

Cassandra pauses. "But would also contravene the laws of the land, not to mention my uncle's views, on women and learning," she says quietly.

Sir Garrick shuffles sideways on the wall, placing the board between them. "I have always thought," he says conversationally, opening the pouch and beginning to place pieces on the game board, "that what went on between a betrothed couple was quite the business of that couple. Your uncle upholds the law of the land, it is true, but you will note that few question his living arrangements with Lady Rhoswen, and they offer no explanation. As they should not."

I breathe a sigh of relief, and feel unexpected tears rise at his words.

"Is that so?" Cassandra says, and for the first time since we met four years ago, I hear tentative hope in her voice.

"Indeed," Sir Garrick says, placing the last piece on the board. "And so I would expect it to be in my own marriage. Now, it seems that you are white, my lady. You must make the first move."

There is a long pause. Lady Cassandra looks from the pieces on the board and up to my face. I nod. We have nothing to lose now.

The fact that Sir Garrick did not storm away at first sight of the chessboard allows a tiny kernel of optimism to seed within me. Could it be that this knight she was so determined to flee may be the solution she needs?

Finally, my lady reaches for a pawn, pushing it forward across the board. Sir Garrick mirrors her move quickly. Tucking that errant curl behind her ear, Cassandra bends forward, leaping her knight into position, and I allow myself a small smile as Sir Garrick again mirrors her move. She is playing a classic opening that my father taught me when I was very young.

As Cassandra slides her bishop up to face off against Sir Garrick's row of pawns, I watch him lean in as he realizes that she has more skill than he had imagined.

I feel a hand under my elbow, and Reeve draws me away.

"Ha!" I hear Cassandra exclaim as Reeve and I fade behind the shrubbery.

"She won't beat him, will she?" Reeve asks, and I think he's only half joking.

"She will if she can," I respond. "My lady is nothing if not competitive. But she is also a relative beginner. The good Sir Knight's pride should remain intact . . . for now."

Reeve smirks. "You would beat him," he says, and there is no question in his voice.

"In a heartbeat," I reply, with a courteous bow and a tiny smile.

"So," he says, dropping to the lush grass and stretching out in the golden, late-afternoon sun. "What do we do now?"

I stand over him, hands on hips. "Technically, we should loll around in the sun, deliberately averting our gaze from our charges whilst keeping their virtue safe."

Reeve snorts, squinting up at me in the bright light. "I sense a 'but.'"

"We have a job to do," I say. "And little time in which to do it."

"Do you have a plan?" He sounds doubtful but is getting to his feet.

I peer around the shrubbery. Cassandra and Sir Garrick are deep into their game, oblivious to their surroundings.

"One of us needs to stay nearby, in case someone comes and catches them playing," I say. I can hardly believe my words, that my mistress's reputation is as much in danger from playing a game as it would be if Sir Garrick were to suddenly ravish her among the flower beds.

"The other must go to the stables to see if they can find out . . . anything."

"Anything?" Reeve says, and his lips quirk. "Could you be more specific?"

To stop myself from punching him, I cross my arms. "Anything," I repeat. "Was Sullivan followed? Did anyone happen to disappear at the same time? Was anyone hanging around the stables that shouldn't have been? Actually, you know what, you stay here and I'll go. At least I'm taking this seriously."

"No, wait," Reeve says, grabbing my flowing skirt as I stomp past him. "You stay here. If anyone comes, it will be Lady Cassandra who will need help, not Sir Garrick. I'll go – and I promise that I will be as thorough and, er, serious as you would be."

I consider. He is right about Cassandra needing me.

"Very well," I say, and Reeve is gone before I have a chance to add anything else.

To my horror, it is but moments before I hear raised voices drifting over from the chess game. I rush to the Lady Cassandra. "Is all well, my lady?" I ask, hoping my expression masks my concern.

"Well, no, Maven, it's not. This cad has just wiped my king from the board." Her voice is bright with merriment.

Sir Garrick holds up his hands in mock surrender. "The lady fought bravely and well," he says, his eyes twinkling. "I just got lucky."

I smile, unsure of my role in this lighthearted banter, but eager to grasp more time for Reeve to make his enquiries. "Perhaps another battle might allow my lady the opportunity to recover her honor?"

"What say you, good Sir Knight?" Cassandra says, and her flushed, excited face is more beautiful than I have seen it in many moons.

"Enchanted," says Sir Garrick, and his expression suggests that he does not lie, although Cassandra is so busy arraying her chess pieces that I suspect she does not see it.

As the game begins, little is heard beyond the click of chess pieces and an occasional murmur, and so I wander toward the entrance to the walled garden. If I stand beside the wooden door, I can ensure that no one enters without warning.

I lean against the warm stones, listening to the rise and fall of chatter as people pass by outside the door.

"Well, I told him that it would snow at midsummer before he'd ever . . ."

"I thought it a fine courser until I saw . . ."

I sink to the grass, spreading my skirts beneath me and, with one last glance in the direction of Sir Garrick and Cassandra, happy to rest for a moment when I know I will not miss the ratchet of the latch that secures the gate.

Time passes, but I hear no shout from the direction of the chessboard. It seems that Cassandra is making Sir Garrick work harder for his victory this time, and I feel a surge of pride.

My ears prick up at the sound of whispering outside the gate. I am able to make out only that it is a man's voice doing most of the talking, with a woman responding briefly. I get to my feet and creep to the gate, dropping so that my ear is in line with the square handhold cut into the door.

"I cannot," I hear the woman's voice say, or, more likely, a girl's.

"You must," comes the gruff response. "If not tonight then never."

The girl gasps, and I hear her begin to sob. "Don't say that, you do not give me orders." I am startled to recognize Lady Anice's brittle tones, although they are less strident when soaked with tears.

The man laughs, harsh and knowing. "Tell me that you would allow me to go without you."

There is a silence. "You pledged your love," Anice says.

"It is mine to pledge and mine to take." His ruthless statement startles me. Who would dare speak so to the Lady Anice?

Then he continues, smooth and wheedling. "Come now, let us retire to the garden."

I freeze as a hand begins to reach through the handhold to lift the latch. I whirl about, ready to run to the Lady Cassandra, but I see that my sharp movements have alerted her, and Sir Garrick is already taking action, deftly flipping the entire chessboard over the wall into the garden beyond while Cassandra rearranges her skirts.

I slow my pace to a genteel stroll, and greet my lady loudly by name. I suspect that whomever it is whispering outside the gate will no more welcome the sight of other people than we would have done a few moments ago.

My thoughts are confirmed when I hear the latch clank back into place, and the gate remains shut.

"It seems we have lingered long enough here," Cassandra says to me when I reach her side. "It is time for me to dress for dinner."

Sir Garrick stands before her and bows. "I look forward to seeing you at table, my lady," he says, and lays a sweet kiss on her hand.

Cassandra smiles at him. "I will also welcome your presence — even if my actions do not necessarily show my joy."

I smile inwardly, applauding her strategy. Cassandra has been won over here today by this clever knight, but she will not allow the Airl to see that.

"It is as much to protect you as me," she continues when Sir Garrick would quiz her. "I am a less valuable proposition to the Airl without the Fire Star, and if he sees value in a friendship between us — or more specifically breaking it up — he will do so."

Sir Garrick appears thoughtful. I wonder that she trusts him with these words, given his many years of loyalty to the Airl, but he quickly repays the favor.

"Very well, my lady, then I shall look forward to another quiet moment between us on the morrow."

As Sir Garrick makes his way to the gate, Cassandra's eyes linger on his upright figure and I find myself wondering at both her absorbed expression and the bond that has formed so quickly here today.

I cannot help but think that, even if Reeve has found the Fire Star hidden in the stable straw, the Lady Cassandra might now have plans of her own.

CHAPTER FIFTEEN

Reeve needed a cool drink, sooner rather than later. After nearly an hour of deftly avoiding the twitchy hind legs and eager teeth of the Airl's string of fine horses as he tried to delicately question every man and boy working in the hot, dusty stables, Reeve's throat was parched and his lips were dry.

Worst of all, he'd discovered nothing. None of the regular stable hands knew much about Sullivan at all. Not that he'd asked about the man by name – there was no way he wanted to be remembered at any stage as having asked about a dead man.

He wasn't entirely sure what Myra had meant when

she'd said she'd "tend" to poor Sullivan, but Reeve knew it was best if his queries remained as oblique as possible. Reeve also knew, however, how to talk to people, and he knew how to turn a general conversation about the quality of a bridle into a discussion about those who worked in the stables.

Reeve knew to find out a little bit from each individual, and then build that into a complete picture.

Unfortunately, the picture he'd built was . . . patchy. Like a stained glass window with broken panes.

He'd learned that there was a new man called Sullivan and that he'd kept to himself. Everyone Reeve had spoken to could recall Sullivan being present in the stables the previous morning, and they'd all been relieved when he'd offered to sweep up the manure in the courtyard.

"It were fresh, you know," one scruffy stable boy had confided, pinching the end of his sharp nose in case Reeve missed the point. "Shouldna' been there but the Lady Anice insisted on another of those early morning rides she suddenly loves so much."

Reeve had bit his lip thoughtfully as he'd considered the information. When she'd been at Harding Manor, Anice had rarely emerged from her chambers before noon, and most of the household had been happy with this. Asleep, she was just bearable; awake, she was an irritable, irascible shrew.

"It is good that the Lady Anice has taken to riding," Reeve had said, keeping his tone light. "It is such a pleasant pastime."

"Gah!" the stable boy had scoffed. "I don't think it's the riding that she's finding pleasant."

Reeve had pretended interest in the stitching on a saddle hanging from the hook beside him. "Goes on her own, does she?"

The boy had laughed again. "Well, she'd 'ave us believe she does," he'd said, laying one finger down the side of his nose, and winking.

Having seen the Lady Anice and Brantley for himself, Reeve had needed no further details. But the fact that the couple had been so indiscreet in their courting that the servants were talking about it bothered Reeve deeply. The Lady Rhoswen would be horrified.

"Oi!" A hoarse whisper brought Reeve from his thoughts. "You after Sully?"

The man leaning against the water barrel in the deepening shadows didn't look as though he worked in the stables, nor indeed anywhere at Rennart Castle. He wore a ragged shirt that might have once been white, ripped breeches and no shoes. He took a sip from a brown pottery crock, one of two by his side, and Reeve caught a whiff of cider as he walked toward the man.

"You know this man called Sully?" Reeve asked, careful not to confirm that he was "after" anyone, and to speak in the present tense.

The man nodded eagerly. "He brought me here," he slurred, slurping at the crock once more. "Found me on the road, he did, and said he could get me a meal. Good man, Sully."

Reeve squatted down beside the man, waving away the proffered crock, despite his powerful thirst. "Did you see him this morning?"

The man studied Reeve a moment. "Who's asking?"

"Reeve of Norwood."

"And why do you want to know?"

Aware that this conversation was far too direct, Reeve scrambled for a reason.

"I am squire to Sir Garrick, Knight Protector of Rennart Castle," he said with as much dignity as he could manage, given his awkward position, deciding to opt for something near the truth. "I am charged with finding out what I can about this morning's theft."

To his surprise, the man started laughing, to the point where he spat cider down his own shirt. "That's an awful lot of title for one so young," he finally managed before sticking out one grubby hand. "Well, Reeve of Many Words, I'm Kit. Just Kit."

Reeve took Kit's calloused hand and shook it. "Nice to meet you, Kit," he said, aware that time was ticking away. "So, did you see, er, Sully this morning?"

Kit leaned back on the barrel. "I did. He told me to

wait here while he swept the courtyard – he were going to get me a new shirt today and some boots. My sister lives in Cleeland, see, and I'm going to see her, see if she has work for me. She'll have work, but will that brute she married let her hire me?"

As Kit prattled on about his sister's "oaf of a husband," Reeve waited impatiently for a gap in the flow of words.

"And did Sully come back with the shirt?" Reeve inserted as soon as Kit drew breath.

"Oh, no," Kit muttered. "He swept the courtyard, came back with two crocks and told me to stay here. He had to go and see someone, and then he'd be back and we could go to my sister's."

"Do you know where he went?" Reeve asked quickly, before the insufferable husband made another appearance.

"That way," said Kit, waving toward the gate with one hand while lifting the crock with another.

"Was he alone?" Reeve probed, his mouth feeling even drier as he watched cider drip down Kit's chin.

Kit paused mid sip, wiping his face with his grubby sleeve. "Why do you care so much about Sully? He's a good man and had nothing to do with anything. I'll vouch for that."

Reeve took a deep breath, affecting nonchalance.

"I'm just wondering," he said, brushing straw from his breeches.

"Your lot does an awful lot of wondering," Kit said before taking another long pull at the crock. "Like that Neale. Know him? He's got a title almost as long as yours."

Reeve froze. "You know Neale of Broadfield?"

"We've met," said Kit, and his tone suggested the meeting hadn't been a happy one.

"When did you last see him?" Reeve asked, and now he gave no pretense of disinterest.

Kit stared at him. "Last night. He came down here asking questions about those two women who rode in late, what guests were expected for the wedding . . . Always asking questions, that one, wanting to know who was where and doing what with whom. Very interested in the comings and goings of Lady Anice's horse."

He stopped, looking Reeve over disapprovingly. "Lots of wondering. Bit like you."

Reeve's thoughts were spinning. Neale had known about the Lady Anice and Brantley. He must have! Why else would he be questioning stable staff about her horse? But if he knew, why had he kept it to himself? What did he hope to gain?

And what else had he discovered? Why the interest in the wedding guests? In Lady Cassandra?

"You okay?" Kit was peering at him.

"Did Neale speak to Sully?" Reeve asked, trying to connect pieces of the puzzle.

"What? No. Sully and me were too lowly for the likes of him to address," Kit scoffed. "He spoke to the Master of Grooms, who gave him short shrift. Nobody down here likes a shrinking, shirking spy."

"A spy?" Reeve said, ears pricked. "That's a strong word to use in these times."

Kit stared at him, balefully. "I speak it as I see it, young Master of All the Titles. He were a spy."

"For whom?" Reeve asked.

"Now, that I don't know," Kit said, leaning back on the barrel. "I ain't been here long enough to know. But Sully . . . he figured it out. I could tell."

Reeve stood up, feeling his muscles protest as he did. "How could you know that?"

"Recognized him, didn't he? First night we were here, Neale was skulking about and Sully kind of faded into the shadows, making sure he kept his face from the light. Says to me that a man recognizes someone and doesn't want to be recognized in return."

Reeve thought a moment. "Did Sully say where he knew Neale from?"

"Nope," said Kit, wiping his hand across his lip to catch some dribble. "And I didn't ask. Speaking of which, I reckon you've asked enough of me, Squire of All the Things. We're starting to attract attention, and I don't need it. I'm just going to wait here for Sully, and then we'll be on our way."

Looking around, Reeve could see Kit was right – two grooms were whispering outside a loose box, throwing glances his way.

"One last thing," Reeve said to Kit, trying to look as though he were stretching his muscles and not interrogating a man. "Did you see anyone follow Sully from the gates this morning?"

Kit laughed. "Only half the castle," he said. "He left after chapel, and you know how busy that is."

Reeve's heart sank. It was true that a crowd of people went through the gates each morning after the chapel service ended. Even the alert guards at the gates wouldn't be able to pick one out.

"Well, thank you, I must go now to assist Sir Garrick at table," he said to Kit. As he did so, he was struck by the poignancy of the man's situation. Kit was waiting for a man who would never show up. A man who had promised to help him toward a brighter future.

"Er, Kit," Reeve continued, thinking fast. "If for any reason Sully doesn't come back by sundown, go to the wyld woman in the woods. She will help you."

Kit eyed him with suspicion. "And why would she do that? She don't know me from a block of tallow."

"She is a good woman. Give her my name and all will be well," Reeve promised with a sureness he did not feel. Hopefully, Maven could use whatever means of messaging she had at her disposal to ask Myra to help Sully's friend.

Kit grunted. "All right, then."

As Reeve walked away, he heard the slosh of cider in the crock once more.

CHAPTER SIXTEEN

The din in the Great Hall is so loud that I cannot imagine that anyone can hear anyone else at all, and yet I see the conversations, here bellowed, there whispered under cover of the fiddle player and his lively airs. At the top table, Lady Cassandra continues to play the part of affronted, rebellious niece, and if I notice her sneaking sideways glances at Sir Garrick it is only because I know her well.

Nearby to me, a red-faced minor lord calls a serving maid for his pigeon-chested, sour-faced lady who is overdressed in last year's fashion, before turning back to the chubby nobleman beside him. I am standing at the back of the hall, among the less desirables on the wedding guest list. These are the people invited out of duty, and so they've arrived too early, eager to curry favor or overindulge in the Airl's hospitality.

It is these people, I know, who will talk too loud or too long about their grievances, and therefore give away more information than they might imagine.

The wall tapestry is rough against my back as I lean on it, and I catch Reeve's eye and smirk, secure in the knowledge that he must stand straight and still behind Sir Garrick and therefore not react. I know, though, that he is listening to all that is said at the top table and will share it with me later. We have agreed to meet outside the kitchens after we have performed all our duties, and I yawn as I realize that, thankfully, the time is near.

I turn to take in the crowded tables once more, my focus drawn to the surly group of young men who have been banished to the very back corner of the hall. I recognize them as the same disreputable group ejected from the hall last night, and realize that the scruffy face of the one Reeve called Brantley is missing.

I wonder idly if he has been banned from table altogether as I follow the unhappy, longing glances each man at the table throws across the hall at a table of sparkling young maidens, decked out in bright silks and feathers.

This is the Lady Anice's coterie, seated beneath the

Airl's watchful eye – the Airl's frowning, watchful eye, I realize, as I catch him taking note of the empty seat at the head of the table. It seems the Lady Anice has absented herself, and the Airl whispers to Sir Garrick.

To my surprise, Reeve is called forward, bending in close as Sir Garrick speaks to him. Around me, the shrieking laughter and hubbub continues, and I know that no one else has noticed the exchange. As Reeve bows and moves without hesitation toward the nearest door, I stand upright.

Sir Garrick has sent him to enquire after the Lady Anice, and I feel my own curiosity rise. I glance across at the table of unhappy young men again and catch them whispering together, staring at the tall candles in the middle of their table. Is it my imagination, or does the central one have a mark upon it, not far below the flame?

My mouth goes dry, remembering the snatch of conversation I'd heard through the garden door earlier that afternoon. Surely, the Lady Anice would not be silly enough to follow a man like Brantley? She is a spoiled and petulant child, it is true, but a scandal like this would be the undoing of her.

Even as I have the thought, I know it to be true. She who has been cosseted and protected her whole life would never imagine that another person would harm her. She is lucky enough to have never had the lesson that I've learned so well.

I gather up my skirts and dart for the closest door, knowing that those around me are too absorbed in stuffing their faces and guzzling their cider to take any notice.

The hallways are no quieter than the hall, filled as they are with serving staff and drunken revelers who have taken the opportunity to engage in more private discussions and assignations. But I have no thought beyond finding Reeve and staving off disaster.

If the Lady Anice departs tonight with a cunning, impoverished blaggard who cannot even afford to buy a knighthood, the Airl's wedding plans will be thrown into disarray, and the whiff of scandal will envelop all at Rennart Castle for a long time to come.

There is no sign of Reeve in the hallway and, if I am not to grind my teeth to the bone in frustration, I realize I must act alone. I turn on my heel, colliding with a footman carrying a full platter of jellied eels. I do not stop to apologize, racing headlong toward the kitchen.

As I run, I try to collect my thoughts. I know that Anice will have left the castle proper, for Brantley will have arranged to meet her somewhere he can get her alone. But where?

When I think of the heated whispers I overheard today, I know that Anice has not committed to leave with him. Brantley may have convinced her to slip away from dinner, but I don't think she would have agreed to go beyond the castle gates. Not yet.

I try to put myself in Brantley's shoes. He is a desperate, angry man and will leave nothing to chance. I do not think he will harm her, but he is thinking only of himself and what he wants. And what he wants is to compromise her good name, tying her to him forever, and therefore ensuring her father's benevolence – or some form of it – toward him.

If he succeeds in compromising the Lady Anice's honor or, even worse, *marrying* her, the Airl will stop at nothing to save the situation, and Brantley will win his knighthood, and her dowry, which is no doubt worth a small fortune – even without the Fire Star.

He will leave nothing to chance. I think of the whispering young men in the Great Hall, watching the candle at their table burn down, and can only hope that I am mistaken about what the mark might signify. My thoughts whirl around as I push past the armies of serving maids who are now leaving the kitchen with platters of sweetmeats and fruit.

Dessert is on its way, which means that I have little time left. The Airl will not allow his daughter to be absent beyond the serving of the last course and will turn the castle upside down to find her.

I need to find Anice first and restore her to the feast, untouched, her reputation unsullied. It is the only way to keep the Lady Cassandra's wedding on course and keep us from being in the nunnery by tomorrow.

The only place I can think to go is the knot garden, with its walls offering protection from prying eyes for a couple planning a rendezvous – yet close enough should one half of the couple wish to be "stumbled" upon.

I reach the door to the courtyard and skid to a halt, my skirts swirling around me as I reach for the handle.

"And where might you be going?"

I have no time for Lorimer right now, but I take a deep breath to calm myself before turning to face him. His dour expression tells me that any story I concoct will need to be a good one.

"It is not seemly for young women to be running through the castle halls after dark," Lorimer continues, turning from me. "Particularly when everyone else is at table. Come with me now. I must write up your indiscretion in the book."

I bite my lip to hold back the curses against this uptight busybody, a stickler for the rules when it suits him. Anger will not help me now.

"Good sire, my Lady Cassandra has sent me to –" I begin, groping about in my mind for a thread. I catch sight of a wooden bucket, full of wilting pink roses beside the door . . .

"Gather roses," I continue, looking away from the bucket even as he turns back to me.

"Roses?" Lorimer says, sniffing at the idea. "Right

now? In the dark?"

"Well, er, yes," I prevaricate. "She wishes to take a rose bath after dinner and . . . well, you know what her whims can be like."

For once I am grateful for Cassandra's reputation as a demanding mistress. Lorimer considers my words. "And yet there are roses by the door," he says, walking over and picking up the bucket. "There are petals here enough to fill my lady's bath."

He hands the bucket to me and I can do nothing but take it from his gloved hand.

"I, well, that is to say . . ." I begin, staring into the bucket at the thorny stems. Tucked right at the bottom, all but buried by green and faded pink, is one tiny white bud.

"They need to be white," I say, as inspiration strikes. "These are pink, and my lady has requested white. So, you see, I must go."

Without giving him a chance to respond, I shove the bucket back at him and run to the door, ignoring his calls to stop. "Back in a jiffy," I shout, forcing a cheeriness I do not feel, barely pausing to pull the door shut behind me with a bang, before sprinting toward the garden.

As I round the corner to approach the gate, however, my heart sinks.

Someone else is there, bent low, peering through the

handhold to the garden inside.

If Reeve could be anywhere else right now, he would go there. Anywhere. He stooped to peek through the handhold again, hoping that the view had changed.

Alas, it had not. He was still observing Brantley and the Lady Anice in a close embrace – which put Reeve in a terrible position. If he was to obey Sir Garrick and "fetch the Lady Anice from wherever she is," he would need to enter the garden, making him a witness to their behavior – behavior that would surely rank at the top of a list of things that the Airl would not wish to hear about right now.

But . . . was it his imagination or did the Lady Anice appear to be struggling within Brantley's embrace? Brantley was holding her closely in his arms, whispering ardently into her ear, one hand on her face. So far, so loverly.

But when Reeve's scrutiny moved down toward her feet, a different story emerged.

"What are you doing?"

Reeve jumped at Maven's fierce voice in his ear even as relief flooded through him. "Am I glad to see you!" he countered, realizing as he spoke how true the words were. "She doesn't want to be there."

As Reeve spoke, he realized that Maven probably had no idea who or what he was talking about, but she didn't hesitate.

"Anice? How can you tell?"

"Her feet are pointed toward the gate, not toward him," Reeve said, earning himself a strange look, but Maven leaned to peep through the gate before straightening up.

"We have to act fast," she said. "Brantley's friends are on their way here, no doubt to 'surprise' the couple. If they catch them like this, Anice will have no choice but to accept a betrothal to save her reputation. We need to get her out of there before the others arrive."

Reeve groaned. "We can't do that without providing him with a witness. He only needs one person to see them embracing to make a betrothal binding. The Airl will be livid with both of us if we give Brantley what he needs to force a marriage."

"We won't give it to him," Maven said, and he was cheered by the determined steel in her voice. "But we must extricate her. If I get her through the gate, can you take her back to the Great Hall without having to go through the kitchens?"

"I think so," Reeve said. "I don't think she came down that way. Brantley would have, to ensure he was seen, but she is not that foolish. Which means she knows a discreet way back."

"I have no comment on her wits," Maven said. "But good point."

Reeve put a hand on her shoulder. "I don't understand how you plan to rescue her without him seeing you."

"He'll see me," Maven replied with a small smile, "but I will not see him."

With those words, she shrugged off his hand and, reaching through, lifted the latch on the gate, pausing a moment before stepping inside and then pulling the gate behind her.

Reeve glanced warily around him. The inner ward of the courtyard was quiet under a big, fat moon, the light of which picked out a handful of servants going about their business. Torches flickered from sconces dotted around the walls, but they served more as decoration under the full moon than necessary sources of light.

A crash rang out from the stables, followed by a bellow, and Reeve wondered briefly if Kit had followed his advice and sought out Myra when Sully did not appear. Maven had promised a message would be sent, and Reeve hadn't asked how.

A door opened somewhere further down the covered walkway that ran along the side of the keep walls. Reeve heard the low buzz of voices before the door closed with a sharp click. Pressing himself flat against the garden wall, he peered into the yawning darkness of the walkway but could see nothing. The moonlight did not reach far enough into the recesses to illuminate anyone lurking there.

Reeve could only hope that whatever Maven had planned, she would be able to carry it out soon. It would not do for any of them to be found skulking around the walled garden in the dark.

My mother and my sisters have always said that my face is so blank that the monks could write psalms upon it, and I can only hope that their words, said in barbed jest, are, in fact, true. For success tonight will depend on it.

As the gate latches behind me, I breathe in the night air, taking in the sweet scent of orange blossom and honeysuckle underpinned by the heady perfume of the roses. Then, keeping my pace measured, I glide toward the knot at the center of the garden, where I can hear Brantley whispering fiercely to Lady Anice, who is struggling to free herself from his grasp.

Inwardly, I curse this horrible man who would hold a girl against her will for his own gain, but, outwardly, I show nothing, strolling as though I have all the time in the world.

In moments, I am upon them, and I do not miss

Brantley's expression of glee. This is what he wants, a witness to his embrace with Lady Anice, someone to support his claim that she is compromised, and, for it to be me, someone totally unconnected to either of them, must look like a heaven-sent opportunity. I must act quickly to ensure that I am the *only* one who sees them together, and I suspect that I have only minutes before the agreed time at which his cronies will "stumble" upon them.

"Ah, Lady Anice," I say, ignoring Brantley. "I have been searching everywhere. The Airl seeks your company at the top table."

I hold out my hand toward her, and she reaches for it like a drowning woman. Her copper hair, so artfully arranged with plaits and curls not half an hour before, is a tangled mess, and her fine features are streaked with tears.

But Brantley will not give up that easily.

"She is busy," he crows, trying to clutch Anice closer. "You can see that. You are witness to our love."

I stare only at Anice, willing her to catch on. "Come now, my lady. I know the scent of the garden is intoxicating, but duty first."

The listless Anice gapes at me as Brantley tightens his grip. I pretend not to notice that she is corralled in his embrace; instead, I smile at her as though

I have caught her dancing barefoot under the stars — alone.

"Hello?" Brantley shouts, waving a hand in my face. "I told you *she is busy*."

But my presence has revived her, and Anice begins to struggle in earnest. It takes everything within me not to step forward and drag her from his arms and this place, but I cannot. The only way out of this is if she is not *seen* with him.

And so, I will not *see* him.

"Oh no you don't," he says, as Anice kicks out at him, shaking her head from side to side and trying to wrest her body from his grip. "This maid may be a dullard, but she has witnessed our love. There's no point in running now. Not when my friends will join us to celebrate our betrothal any minute. They will back up my claims that you have agreed to my proposal."

At his words, I see her panic grow as the reality of his plans — and her plight — set in. I know I must act if we are to get away in time.

With his attention on Anice, I begin to ease myself around them until I am standing behind Brantley. Anice can see me and, at my nod of encouragement, continues to struggle, increasing her efforts until they are all but wrestling.

"Ouch! That hurt, you cow!"

With one huge sideways movement, Anice manages

to knock him off balance, and that's when I step in with a giant shove that topples him. "Run, my lady," I shout, trying to keep out of his arm's reach as she picks up her skirts. "That's right. Hurry! Your father awaits!"

I have still not acknowledged Brantley's presence, or the situation, in words, but I grab at his leg as he tries to roll under Anice's feet to trip her. He thrusts his foot back at me, catching me on the side of the face. For a moment, the world wobbles and I let go of his leg, backing away and trying to catch my breath.

He is spitting with rage, glowering at me, but does not get up to chase after Anice, who by now has reached the gate. "Ha!" he says. "It's too late anyway. You saw us."

In response, I walk over to a huge rosebush, so laden with frilly white blooms that its branches droop and the grass below it is strewn with petals. "Just what I was looking for," I say, managing to sound almost normal, even though my jaw is aching. "Lady Cassandra will love these."

I unsheathe my knife and pull it from my pocket, making sure that Brantley sees the gleam of the blade in the moonlight, feeling a spurt of relief as he backs out of reach. Swiftly, I cut six blooms on long stems from the bush, ignoring the sting of the thorns in my fingertips. Then, as though I am quite alone, albeit with my knife still held aloft, I turn back to the gate, not favoring Brantley with so much as a sideways glance.

I walk away from him at the same, steady pace at which I entered, not quite turning my back.

"Hey!" he shouts. "Hey! Answer me, wench."

But I will not. If I cannot see him, I cannot hear him and I will not answer him. My aching jaw reminds me that I will have a bruise to explain on the morrow, and that it may be used against me.

But one bruise looks much like another.

As I reach the gate, I slip the knife back into my pocket and call out to Reeve in an undertone. As I expect, he pushes hard against the gate just as I arrive at it, catching me full in the face with a bang as he does so.

"Gads!" Reeve says loudly. "I'm sorry! I did not realize you were so close. Are you all right?"

Holding my cheek, I look past his concerned face to where Brantley's posse is emerging from the kitchen door. They slouch toward the garden, elbowing each other in anticipation of Brantley's plan.

"I'm fine," I say, even louder, as I slide through the narrow gate and watch as the approaching men hesitate. "I was just collecting roses in the empty garden and I seem to have walked into the gate."

Brantley's friends look at each other, frowning, before turning as one and walking away back to the kitchen, their muttered conversation growing louder with every step.

"What did you just do?" Reeve asks me, his brow furrowed.

"Did the Lady Anice get away?" I whisper, leaning against the garden wall as my poor, sore head spins. Reeve nods.

"Did she see you?" I ask, and he shakes his head.

"I didn't think I'd be a welcome sight," Reeve admits. "So I hid when I saw her coming through the gate."

I allow myself a small smile. "Then we did it. I must go to her now and help fix her appearance so she can return to the feast at once."

I turn toward the kitchen door.

"Where are you going?" he asks. "Anice went that way." He points into the darkness of the covered walkway.

I wave my roses at him. "I need to walk past Lorimer with these," I say, not waiting for his response as I stride away.

CHAPTER SEVENTEEN

Friday

How Maven had done it, Reeve did not know, but just as the last revelers in the Great Hall were leaning back in their seats, patting their stomachs and loosening their belts, the Lady Anice had slid into her seat beneath her father's intense and angry gaze, not an errant hair out of place.

Reeve had watched as one of Anice's companions had leaned across the table, giggling and whispering, only to recoil when Anice spoke to her in low tones. Whatever it was she said, it had the effect of dampening the spirits of the entire table, who had then sat in polite silence for a few more minutes before standing almost as one and filing demurely from the room.

Lady Anice had made a great show of curtseying to her father before mounting the raised platform on which the top table sat and placing a loving goodnight kiss on his red, wrinkled forehead, and a white rose into his hand.

During all of this, Maven had been nowhere to be seen, and Reeve could only imagine she'd gone to place a cool cloth on her face. He still felt bad about the force with which he'd opened the garden gate, and could only hope that she would not be bruised.

Now, having served Sir Garrick his breakfast, Reeve's glance sought her out. The turnout for breakfast this morning was light, which was unsurprising given that last night's feast had rolled on well into the early hours once the tables had been pushed back and the fiddler given center stage.

The Lady Cassandra had excused herself not long after Anice, leaving the Airl and Sir Garrick to their business. Reeve had noticed that both had drunk sparingly as they'd greeted the long line of men who'd taken it in turns to fill the empty seats at their table, airing one grievance or another, or using the cover of the fiddler's wild melodies for low-voiced conversation.

As the candles had spat and guttered and the fiddler had turned his hand to aching ballads of loss and forgiveness, the group around the Airl had stabilized into a handful of lean, hardened men, and the discussion had become intense and quietly heated.

Reeve had been relieved when, finally, Sir Garrick had turned to him. "You may as well go to bed, Reeve," he'd said. "Tomorrow will be another long day, and I have no need of you here."

"I would take the duty of the Squire of the Body, sire," Reeve had answered, stifling a yawn but knowing his duty. "You will need assistance in Neale's absence."

Sir Garrick had demurred. "You have done enough today, Reeve," he'd said, and Reeve had blushed at the acknowledgement. "I can take my own boots off, but I will need you bright and lively on the morrow."

Reeve had bowed and backed away, but he'd noticed that, as he did so, the Airl, Sir Garrick and the surrounding men had leaned in close, ignoring those slumped over scattered tables across the Hall.

Now, Reeve stood back in his place behind Sir Garrick, who was picking at the fruit in his trencher with little interest. The Airl, too, was slow to eat, though Reeve suspected he was more alert behind his heavy-lidded eyes than he was letting on. Certainly, he stiffened as a pale-looking Anice entered the hall, her companions trailing behind her, their faces still creased with sleep.

"You are up early today, my daughter," the Airl said as she took her customary seat.

"I could not sleep," Anice answered, not looking at her father.

"How so?" said the Airl. "Are you troubled?"

Anice raised her eyes to her father, and Reeve saw her swallow before she answered. "Not in the least," she said, and Reeve thought she was just convincing enough, though anyone looking for it would see the brittleness of her smile.

The Airl merely harumphed before mopping some soft-boiled egg from his plate with a hunk of bread. Fortunately, the Lady Cassandra chose that moment to enter, a bewitching vision in a deep-blue gown, her hair piled up to frame her face.

But it was not *her* face that made Reeve gasp out loud.

A few paces behind Lady Cassandra, already making for her favored position along the back wall, Maven kept her head down, but even so Reeve could see the deep purple bruise that bloomed across her jawline. His mouth went dry. Could the accident with the gate be responsible for that?

"Good morning," trilled the Lady Cassandra. "I see we are all awake early this morning. How fortuitous it is to have a chance to discuss the missing Fire Star."

The Airl's expression darkened but, before he had a chance to respond, there was a disturbance at the door. Brantley marched in, flanked by the men that Reeve had seen in the courtyard the night before.

"Ah!" Brantley said, stumbling over a chair as he made a beeline for the Lady Anice. "There she is! My beloved! My betrothed!"

Anice jumped to her feet, as pale as winter snow, her ladies flocking to her side, trying to create a polite wall between Anice and Brantley. But he was not to be deterred, pushing them out of the way before grasping Anice around the waist.

"What is the meaning of this?!" the Airl thundered, his fist pounding the table so hard that his plate rattled on the wood.

Sir Garrick thrust back his chair to stand beside the Airl, his hand automatically reaching for his sword, which, as per Great Hall protocol, was not there.

"Why, did she not tell you?" Brantley asked with a wild laugh, one arm waving above his head, playing to his cronies, the other gripping Anice. "Your daughter and I are betrothed."

"You are no such thing, you upstart," growled the Airl. "My daughter would not be so foolish as to hitch herself and her good name to a blaggard such as you."

"And yet she met me in the knot garden last night while you were at table," said Brantley. "Tell them, sweet, tell them how we embraced under the stars with the scent of roses around us."

It was too much for Anice, who swooned into a dead faint in Brantley's arms. Staggering under the sudden weight, he shoved Anice's slight figure toward her friends, who had to rush forward to catch the girl lest she drop to the floor.

"See," Brantley went on, swaggering over to the Airl's table to steal a grape from the platter, a hectic flush of color beneath the stubble on his face. "She is so overcome with love for me that she swoons. It seems we shall have a double wedding on the morrow."

He turned to his friends and popped the grape in his mouth and they gasped, half in horror, half in awe. Reeve was close enough to see the line of sweat along Brantley's hairline and smell the stale scent of cider on his breath.

"You are very certain of yourself," said Sir Garrick, not raising his voice. "So certain that I am sure that you have evidence of your wild . . . accusations."

"Oh, I do," said Brantley, and Reeve wondered at his confidence. "There she is!"

Brantley's long finger pointed at Maven, who did not flinch.

"Your maid, Cassandra?" the Airl thundered, turning a disapproving face toward his niece.

"Indeed," said Lady Cassandra, appearing unperturbed, and Reeve wondered how much Maven had told her of the night before. "Bring her here. I am sure she will clear this up."

Maven left her place at the back of the room and came to stand before Lady Cassandra, the perfect picture of a demure maid. In her serviceable brown dress, with the bruise sweeping her face, her noble roots were not obvious, and Reeve thought that if he did not know her, he would consider Maven of no consequence.

Which, he was beginning to understand, was just how she liked it.

"Yes, my lord?" Maven whispered. The Airl looked down at her bowed head, and seemed unsure of where to begin.

"Perhaps this man could advise us of exactly what it is he thinks my devoted and loyal servant knows about him," Lady Cassandra prompted.

By now, Lady Anice was beginning to come around, muttering to herself, her head cradled by one of her ladies. Reeve saw Maven shoot a loaded glance up at Lady Cassandra.

"Quickly now," Cassandra said to Brantley, clapping her hands with regal grace. "Tell your story and be done with it."

Brantley strutted over to Maven, standing over her as though to intimidate her with his size. When Maven ignored him, he turned to Lady Cassandra, feet spread wide, hands on hips.

"She saw us," he said. "She came into the knot garden last night and witnessed our embrace. Now she must tell."

The Airl was silent for a moment, considering the scruffy squire's bald statement as well as his swooning daughter on the floor.

"Well, girl," the Airl said, sitting back in his tall, carved chair, his voice heavy. "Tell us what you saw."

Maven's smile was sweet when she met his gaze. "Well, I did see the Lady Anice –"

The Airl's groan was audible.

"But I saw only she," Maven went on, speaking to the Airl as though they were the only people in the room. "I went to the knot garden to get some white roses for my Lady Cassandra's bath, and discovered Lady Anice there, enjoying a quiet moment in the night air."

The Airl sat forward as a flurry of whispers echoed around the hall. "Alone?"

"I saw only she," Maven repeated. "I'm sure that, had there been anyone else of consequence in the garden, I would have seen them."

"*You lie!*" roared an incensed Brantley, moving to stand in front of Maven. "I kicked your face! Tell them how you came by that bruise."

Even Sir Garrick looked taken aback at his explosion. "You kicked this girl in the face?"

Brantley seemed to realize what this sounded like. "By accident," he said. "She was trying to stop me –"

He broke off, his expression becoming sullen as

he realized he was doing himself no favors. "Anyway," Brantley said. "It proves she was there."

Maven touched her face. "This?" she said, as though embarrassed. "Reeve of Norwood did this."

Reeve's face burned as attention – and disapproval – shifted to him, but he said nothing. Hearing this story unfold, Reeve was beginning to understand why the Lady Cassandra spoke of Maven's "many talents."

"Oh, not like that," Maven said, with a girlish giggle that Reeve decided he would probably never hear again – unless it served a purpose. "I walked into the gate as I left the garden. Reeve opened it on me."

"Is this true, squire?" the Airl asked, censure warring with hope in his tone.

"Sad to say that it is true, your excellency," Reeve said, putting as much regret into his voice as he could manage while inwardly saluting Maven's courage and strategic planning. "I was looking for Lady Anice, as Sir Garrick asked me to do, and I pushed open the gate just as Maven was leaving, catching her in the face."

"And the Lady Anice?" the Airl probed. "Did you see her in the garden?"

Reeve crossed his fingers behind his back. "I did not enter the garden," he said. After all, technically *he* had not been in the garden when he'd peered through the gate.

Reeve paused, realizing that he was in a position to

assist Maven further. "You could ask them, though," Reeve said, pointing at the pack of youths huddled together, watching Brantley. "I saw them approach the garden, so maybe they saw the Lady Anice?"

All six of Brantley's friends looked as though they wished they could sink into the stone floor as the Airl's dark gaze lowered on them.

"We, er, well, that is to say," began a tall man with a prominent Adam's apple.

"Yes?" said Sir Garrick, one eyebrow raised.

"We didn't see nothing," said another man, and Reeve recognized him as being Derric, the balding man who had nearly felt Brantley's sword on the back of his neck during Reeve's memorable first night at the castle. Now, Derric turned from Sir Garrick to give Brantley a malevolent stare. "Nothing."

Brantley had gone red with anger, all of it directed at Maven. "You lie!" he hissed, while she kept her attention fixed on the Airl. "This is all your fault!"

The Airl sat back in his chair. "I think I've heard enough," he said, lifting his chin toward Sir Garrick, who strode over and grasped Brantley firmly by the arm.

"I will not listen for a moment longer to your tawdry and feeble attempts to besmirch my daughter's good name," the Airl continued, as Brantley tried to wriggle from Sir Garrick's grip. "You are not fit to lick the floor on which she walks and you will not use her to fulfill your sad little ambitions. I henceforth banish you from this castle, and from this kingdom. Sir Garrick, as Knight Protector of Rennart Castle, I hereby order you to accompany this man to the village of Cleeland and put him on the first ship you find that is departing for distant climes."

"No!" gasped Brantley, as Sir Garrick moved to fasten his wrists behind him with a piece of leather thong that he'd pulled from his belt. "You sentence me to death, your excellency. You know you do."

Reeve bit his lip, knowing that Brantley's words were true, knowing that he was, in fact, listening to his own worst nightmare come to life. Ships left Cleeland every day, but few returned. It was the port of choice for adventurers seeking riches, and they ran their ships hard, fast and lean.

"I am giving you the opportunity to make something of yourself," the Airl said, his face tight with anger, and Reeve winced as he heard the echo of his own father's voice in the Airl's words.

Airl Buckthorn stood. "Clearly, you have learned nothing here about chivalry or honor, and you will never be a knight in the kingdom of Cartreff as long as I draw breath, not after what you've attempted here today. Go now!"

As his erstwhile friends watched on, ashen faced, Brantley was dragged, struggling, from the room.

"And Garrick," the Airl called, just before his Knight

Protector disappeared through the door, "be as quick as you can, and keep your ears open in Cleeland."

Sir Garrick sketched a wave and disappeared.

"What happened?" said the Lady Anice, rousing from her stupor on the floor, one feeble hand held to her forehead.

The Airl looked down at his dazed, confused daughter. "Fortunately for you, nothing," he said, and Anice winced at his sternness. "I'm not exactly sure what went on last night, but I suspect that you owe this young lady a great deal. Perhaps you have words for her?"

The Airl gestured toward Maven, whose dark bruise stood out in stark relief on her composed face. Anice was silent for a moment, as though taking in her father's words, before beginning to struggle to her feet.

"My father, forgive me but my head is aching and my thoughts confused. I think I must retire to my rooms for a poultice and some honey water."

The Airl grimaced as everyone else present stared at their feet, embarrassed by Anice's lack of courtesy. "Perhaps it would be best if you stayed there for the rest of the day. Just to ensure you are at your very best for the wedding tomorrow."

Anice fluttered one hand at him. "Perhaps I will," she said, strolling past Maven toward the door with her ladies trailing afterward. "I wouldn't want to appear tomorrow with a bruise on my face, after all. It's so . . . unsightly."

Reeve heard a stifled gasp from the Lady Cassandra, but Maven's expression did not alter. As he watched, she glanced around, as though to see who might hear her words, before speaking.

"Better to be bruised than . . . betrothed," Reeve heard Maven mutter.

Reeve suppressed a smile as Anice tensed, and he wondered if she would respond. But Anice tossed her hair and stalked through the door.

"Well," said the Airl, looking around at those left in the Great Hall. "It seems that we have witnessed an amateurish display of mummerism over breakfast. We can be thankful for just one thing – that the audience for the performance was small. Let us ensure that it remains that way."

His cold stare at Brantley's former friends had them shifting uncomfortably in their house boots.

The Airl clapped. "And now, there is much to do to prepare for tomorrow's festivities. I expect you all to play your part – unless, of course, there are others present who fancy a trip to Cleeland?"

Again, he looked hard at the increasingly restless youths, who all shook their heads sullenly. "Then let us get on with it. You –"

To Reeve's horror, the Airl was pointing at him.

"In Neale's absence, you must go with Sir Garrick to Cleeland. You will find him in the stables, by now, I would think. It is your job to ensure he returns in good time for tomorrow's wedding breakfast. And do not imagine that I have forgotten your other task. Time runs out for you, young squire, and the location of the Fire Star remains unknown."

Reeve managed a small bow, and hurried from the room, feeling Maven's stare upon him. How exactly he was supposed to find the Fire Star at Rennart Castle while he was on the road to Cleeland was a question that the Airl would not welcome at this point.

Feeling helpless, his mind churning, Reeve crossed the courtyard toward the stables, so distracted by his thoughts that he was startled when the castle gates creaked open to admit six riders, all astride huge, snorting black destriers, and all but one dressed in the same green livery.

The lead rider, clad head to toe in black with a deep red traveling cloak that marked him as a member of the nobility, pulled his mount to a sudden halt in the center of the courtyard, slid off his horse and stormed toward the castle, all in one motion, with the other five following suit. A hush descended across the courtyard as everyone stopped to watch what happened next.

To Reeve's surprise, the Airl of Buckthorn himself

emerged from the main doors to greet the party, accompanying the man in the red cloak inside while the other five took up formation behind them.

"Who's that?" Reeve asked, turning to the man in the blacksmith's apron next to him.

"Why, that's Lord Mallor," said the blacksmith, pulling thoughtfully at his graying beard. "I expect he'll be here for the wedding. Pity his son is not here to greet him."

"Son?" said Reeve, distracted by the army of stable boys who'd arrived to tend Lord Mallor's horses.

The blacksmith spat on the cobblestones. "Neale of Broadfield," he said. "Lord Mallor is also known as Airl Broadfield. It gets right confusing, all of those different titles and names, but there you have it."

But Reeve was staring at the pale-green globule glistening at the man's feet. "You don't like Neale?" he asked.

The blacksmith guffawed. "I don't like anyone who asks too many questions," he said, turning to walk away. "And you, my friend, are going to be on that list any minute."

Reeve hesitated before tapping the blacksmith's shoulder. "Neale asked a lot of questions?" he said, remembering what Kit had said about Neale poking around the stables. "What kinds of questions?"

"See now," said the blacksmith, turning back to face

Reeve, muscled arms folded across his barrel chest. "Right there is exactly what I mean. Not just one but two questions."

Reeve smiled in what he hoped was a winning way. "Last ones, I promise," he said, holding up his hands as though in surrender.

The blacksmith wiped his own hands on his heavy apron, adding new streaks of grime to the worn leather. "Questions about how I felt about the King," he said after a moment. "About the Airl's movements. About how many new swords I've been making. About the way I smith Sir Garrick's armor. And that, my friend, is as much as I can tell you."

More questions crowded Reeve's mind as the blacksmith lumbered away toward his forge, but the questions would, Reeve realized, need to wait. It was not only that the blacksmith would not answer them, but that, even as Reeve stood here thinking, Sir Garrick was riding from the stable yard. Behind him, attached by a lead rope, hunched Brantley on a small bay mare, boxed in by Sir Garrick's soldiers on every side.

"Come, Reeve!" Sir Garrick shouted. "Time is a-wasting. Your horse is saddled. Follow now!"

With that, Sir Garrick spurred his charger forward, straight for the still-open gates, with the others clattering behind him. Brantley looked horribly uncomfortable, gagged and, Reeve noticed, with his wrists still tied together, albeit in front to give him some charge of the animal beneath him.

As they hurtled through the gate, Reeve began to run to the stables.

It wouldn't do to get too far behind, and there was much he needed to discuss with Sir Garrick.

CHAPTER EIGHTEEN

"You did well in there, Maven," says Cassandra, her eyes meeting mine in the mirror, voice measured. "Subtle and clever . . . which is more than I can say for the way you are wielding that comb."

I loosen my grip on the offending comb, realizing that I am attacking her knots with the same fervor that I would like to attack Anice for her attitude toward me. Or, indeed, the Airl for confining Cassandra and me to our rooms for "rest" while Reeve gets to gallop off to Cleeland to mete out justice to that villain Brantley, and while the Fire Star is missing.

"I am sorry," I say now, placing the comb carefully on

the dresser and massaging her scalp where I have tugged at her hair. "It's just —"

Her hand reaches up to still one of mine. "I know exactly what it is," Cassandra says. "But subtle and clever is how we have all agreed that it must be played. Until we get what we want."

She pauses. "You did the right thing by the Lady Anice, and she recognizes this, even if her pride will never let her admit it. She is my cousin but . . . she cannot help but think only of herself. You'll note she has not bothered to so much as wish me well since our arrival. Lady Rhoswen would be mortified."

Cassandra sighs as I massage her scalp. "She was wretched to you, but you know the Beech philosophy —"

"Help other women and girls, no matter what," I finish, smoothing her hair. "I know."

I choose three locks of Cassandra's hair and begin to braid their length. We are ostensibly trying hairstyles for her wedding day, but I take no pleasure in the complicated weaving of her dark curls. I wear my own brown hair as simply as possible, and would cut it short like a pageboy if I did not know that it would make me stand out in every room in Rennart Castle. Much better to keep my hair and blend in.

"You will look beautiful tomorrow," I say, changing the subject and watching for her reaction in the mirror. Last night, after we had finally been able to leave the Great

Hall and return to our rooms, Cassandra had talked and talked and talked about Sir Garrick, a veritable waterfall of words that gushed and ran over me as I had lain beside her on the bed, trying to soothe her to sleep. My role as companion is to make her life and mind easier and more comfortable, which means that if she is awake, then I am awake. No matter how much I wish to sleep.

"If I must do this, then I will go to the altar with my head high," Cassandra says now, a faint blush on her cheeks.

I let a beat pass. "Now that you have spent time with Sir Garrick, I wonder if you have changed your mind about the abhorrence of the marriage," I offer, taking another small section of hair to work.

Cassandra exhales sharply. "It is true that he is an . . . interesting man. Marriage to him is a very different proposition than it was to Sir Alfred."

I stifle a chuckle. Given that Sir Alfred was eighty-seven years old, this is something of an understatement.

"But the fact remains that he is not my social equal," Cassandra continues, her reflected face looking thoughtful. "Marrying him will not bring me the status that will lift me above my sisters. Which is something I cannot overlook . . . can I?"

I say nothing, but inside I feel a tiny sinking sensation. As I had thought last night, there has been a distinct softening in her attitude to Sir Garrick. Will she still choose to run if the Fire Star appears before the appointed time of the marriage tomorrow?

I suspect that if I ask her outright she will pooh-pooh me and tell me that she will, but the truth is that marriage to Sir Garrick is a much less risky proposition for a lady like Cassandra than fleeing across the water to a foreign kingdom. No matter what her sisters might say.

And if Cassandra stays, so must I. I have not the means to take flight by myself, and have not yet attained the age at which the Beech Circle will help me. Rules established over many generations of trial and error deem seventeen to be the youngest age whereby girls are able to truly live independently. The Circle would help me to go now, but would place me in another household somewhere in Talleben until I turn seventeen. Why swap one cage for another?

"Have you heard from Myra?" I ask, again changing the subject and concentrating on the pattern of the braid as I work down the length of hair. "Has she any news of the Fire Star?"

Cassandra sighs again. "Not a peep," she says, and, in her reflection, I can see her tears. "It seems it is truly gone for good, and with it our chances of freedom. Now, I must hope that the Airl goes ahead with the wedding regardless, or we are lost to the nunnery forever."

She pauses, her fingers playing with a brass hairpin

on the dresser. "I can't believe it was only days ago that we were flying toward Rennart Castle with wings on our heels, thinking that our plan was foolproof."

I loop the plait before taking the hairpin from her to fix it to her head, saying nothing until I have begun to braid the other side. "We could not foresee murder," I say, as I work the strands of hair. "How could we, when the only people who knew of our plan were we two, Sully and Myra?"

Her eyes narrow in the reflection. "Someone knew," she says. "The question is: how?"

The question is: how?

"Someone saw," I say, knowing that I am repeating Myra's words, just as I have done in my mind over and over. The repetitive action of weaving Cassandra's hair seems to unlock a different, reflective part of my mind, and I continue to speak my thoughts out loud in a way that I have not yet done with her. "Someone in that courtyard saw Sully catch the stone. They murdered him for it."

Cassandra half turns to face me. "But the Airl said that everyone in the castle has been accounted for. Lorimer reports that the stone is nowhere to be found, and says that no one left suddenly after it went missing—even that other squire has not been seen since the night before. You would think, wouldn't you, that if someone had murdered Sully and taken possession of the Fire Star, then they would want to make themselves scarce as soon as possible?"

I reach the bottom of the length of braid before I answer. "Unless," I say, carefully taking a hairpin from the dresser and slipping it into place, "they don't have it."

Her lips twist with disbelief. "What do you mean?" she says, her brow furrowed. "They killed Sully and took the stone from him."

But now my mind is racing as I stare at my own reflection in the mirror. That Sully was murdered and the stone missing were two irrefutable facts. But what if they were actually separate events?

What was it that Reeve had told me about the stables when he'd asked me to send a message to Myra about directing a drunkard to visit her? Something about the other squire, Neale, and all his questions . . .

I watch my reflection frown as I think.

If the drunkard had noticed Neale and all his questions, had Sully? And what were all the questions about? Had Sully seen something or someone that made him wary? And if that were the case, what would he do?

"I think," I say out loud for the first time, walking to the window to look down upon the courtyard, "that Sully hid the Fire Star."

Cassandra twists again in her seat. "Hid it?" she says, and her cheeks are flushed with excitement. "What do you mean?"

"Think about it," I say. "He was to meet Myra and me at the bottom of the road. I think he came empty-handed to keep it safe. That's why he was killed. Not to cover up the theft of the Fire Star, but because *he didn't have it on him* and wouldn't say where it was."

The courtyard below me is a hive of activity, as always. The knights are practicing jousting, thundering toward each other on horses, before pulling aside at the last moment, whooping and yelling.

Anice strolls around the practice ring with a tight knot of her companions, their brightly colored gowns fluttering like butterfly wings in the light breeze. Apparently recovered from her headache, Anice whispers with her friends, not close enough to the male activities to be improper, not far enough away for a girl whose reputation – and future – rested on a knife's edge only hours ago.

I cannot even rouse enough feeling to despise the girl, even though she has survived her unwise decisions unscathed while I am confined to Cassandra's room. I know I have done my duty where Anice is concerned, not that it will ever gain me anything but disdain from her.

I am not interested enough in fashion and flirting to earn Anice's respect.

Sometimes, in quiet moments, I wish that I were different. I wish that I could be like other girls and laugh

233

and flirt and not think about much at all. It all seems to be so much easier when you can just be like everyone else. But I have never been that way, and my father understood it while my mother despised it. Perhaps because she knew how difficult life would be for me. Perhaps because she recognized how difficult it could make life for her.

A flash catches my eye as the sun hits a window near the kitchen door. Lorimer's window, I realize, glad to be drawn from the mire of my own thoughts, and he is framed within it, watching over proceedings in the courtyard. I wonder just how much he sees from his lair. He cannot see all I can see because he's on the ground floor, but he has a clear view of the comings and goings of the kitchen staff in and out of the door. As I watch, he turns from the window, his attention caught by someone in the room behind him.

I turn away.

"What can we do?" Cassandra is saying, her face alight, and it takes me a moment to realize she speaks of the Fire Star. "Can we find it?" She is on her feet, pacing excitedly. "Do you realize what this means? If we can find it, Maven, we can still run."

I watch her for a moment before responding. "My lady, do you still want to?"

Cassandra stands stock-still, one hand over her mouth.

"Forgive me," I rush on, moving toward her. "I do

not mean to question you. It's just that you seemed so very happy with Sir Garrick yesterday afternoon, and he had eyes only for you this morning. It could be that this marriage, with a man who seems open to you pursuing your interests, may be the answer to your prayers — no matter what your sisters think."

"I —" Cassandra sinks upon the bed, her gown settling around her like autumn leaves falling to the ground. "I want to say 'don't be silly.' But I am not entirely certain that I can say those words honestly," she admits.

She looks down at her feet, clad in satin slippers. "I am not like you, Maven. I am not strong, and smart and inexhaustibly resourceful, unbound by what others think of me. I want to be that way, and had Sir Garrick turned out to be the slovenly oik that I had thought him, perhaps I would have found it in me to be so . . . But the truth is that he is . . . interesting to me."

I manage a smile at Cassandra's words, wondering if she understands how much easier it is not to care for what others think of you when the truth is that people *rarely* think of you. "My lady," I say instead, "you are falling in love. There is no greater strength in any person than being open to a new direction."

These are the words my father gave me when he told me he'd secured a position with Cassandra for me, and I'd hated him for them. I acknowledge the irony to myself of using them to bind myself further to that position.

Cassandra bites her lip, suddenly looking much younger than her twenty-five years. "You give me far too much credit, Maven. It feels to me that I am simply stepping onto a well-trodden path."

I sit beside her on the bed. "More foolish to run away from something that will bring you contentment, my lady, and I think that this will do that — more so than being cut off in Talleben from the only life you've ever known."

She takes my hand. "But what of you?" she says softly. "I do not forget the comfort and support you have given me, and I understand that the decision I make now is for both of us."

I take a deep breath. "I am used to changes in direction, my lady," I say, straightening my shoulders. "This is not the first time for me, and look how well the last one worked out."

At least I will give my father that.

Cassandra manages a smile. "You are wise beyond your years, and a great solace to me, Maven. Whatever happens, I will ensure your security."

I jump to my feet so she cannot see the tears that might well up from the hard lump of disappointment I swallow. I will find the Fire Star, for it will secure Cassandra's future, one way or the other.

It will also help Reeve of Norwood to fulfill his ambitions of becoming a knight and, given his knowledge of our secrets, it will be safer to keep him close. What it is that Myra holds over him I do not know, but I cannot count on the fact that it will be enough to stay his tongue if the Fire Star does not turn up and he is ordered from the castle.

He is a charming boy, but his willingness to pull out the chessboard yesterday shows that he is also canny and strategic. If it will save his knighthood to throw me and Cassandra under a cart, I cannot guess at what he will do.

No, working with Reeve to find the Fire Star is the safest course for both of us.

"Maven?" Cassandra's voice is tentative. "Do you know where the Fire Star is?"

"Not exactly," I say, resting my face against the cold, hard window where I have a clear view of dark roiling clouds building in the sky beyond the stables. "But I do know that we're going to need the Beech Circle."

CHAPTER NINETEEN

A long, hard ride. Truer words were never spoken, Reeve thought as his charger barreled along the road beneath him, apparently impervious to the rain that lashed them both in the face. Reeve drew his cloak up over his head more tightly, wincing as his sodden breeches slipped around on the saddle.

He could hear the thunder of Sir Garrick's mount's hooves ahead of him, which was a good thing, for he could barely see beyond the end of his own horse's ears, so thick were the sheets of water falling from the sky.

"Reeve!" Sir Garrick shouted over the drumming of both rain and hooves.

"Here!" Reeve shouted back, as he'd done every few minutes for the past hour. When the rain had begun, Reeve had quietly hoped they'd take shelter under a tree. But that was not how the Knight Protector of Rennart Castle operated.

"Let's get it over with," Sir Garrick had said to Reeve. "The afternoon wears on, and the sooner we get home, the better."

And so they'd ridden, the miles disappearing beneath the galloping horses, leaving Brantley behind on the Cleeland docks, four hefty soldiers on hand to ensure he boarded the ship that was leaving at midnight.

"Not long now!" Sir Garrick shouted again. "We'll see the castle soon enough. They'll have lit the torches early."

Only a cat would see torches in this soup, thought Reeve, trying to snuggle further into his saturated cloak, hoping to find a dry spot somewhere.

But suddenly there was light. A lantern that seemed to swing onto the road, its brightness startling in the sodden darkness. Reeve blinked, pulling hard on his reins, even as he heard Sir Garrick's horse come to a skidding, splashing halt ahead of him.

"Who goes there?" Sir Garrick bellowed, not so much a question as an order for a response. Reeve didn't need to be able to see his master to know that his hand was on the sword buckled to his side.

Reeve squinted, trying to see beyond the dazzling light to the dark figure beyond.

"Stop in the name of the King," came the strident response, and Reeve blinked. The voice sounded familiar but he couldn't quite place it. What was very apparent, however, was the shrill note of anxiety underlying the words.

Sir Garrick's horse danced under him, shifting on the spot. "Well now," the knight said, and Reeve sat up straighter at his friendly tone. "It's good to see you, Neale. Where the devil have you been, boy? We have been worried."

"Do not call me *boy*," Neale said, raising the lantern high so that now Reeve could see his pale, taut face. Rain had plastered Neale's black hair to his head, and his cloak was covered in leaves.

"You look as though you've been crawling about in the shrubbery," said Sir Garrick, sounding amused. "Why don't you climb up behind Reeve and we'll take you to the castle? There are many who've been most anxious about your absence – including your father."

Neale paused, and Reeve felt a prickle along the back of his neck. Something was not right.

"My father knows exactly where I am," Neale said. "I rode for home directly from dinner on Wednesday. I had to let him know you and the Airl of Buckthorn for the traitors that you are. We returned together."

It was Sir Garrick's turn to hesitate, and Reeve swallowed, remembering those quiet conversations he'd overheard between the Airl and his Knight Protector. Had Neale heard those discussions and taken them to his father? His father who had ridden into Castle Rennart that very day with five knights at his side?

Sir Garrick laughed. "To call a man a traitor is to place oneself in the position of having to prove the claim or bear the consequences," he said, and Reeve was again surprised by his conversational tone. Why his master would be settling in for a chat about all this in the pouring rain was beyond Reeve.

"I know what is planned," Neale hissed, and Reeve felt his stomach sink. "And what I know will soon be common knowledge. We will drag the Airl before King Bren's throne and throw him at the royal feet."

"Is that so?" Sir Garrick asked, idly. "And yet what you think you may know and proving what you think you may know are two entirely different matters, are they not?"

As Sir Garrick spoke, Reeve thought he detected a welcome abatement in the solid rhythm of the rain. Still, he could not help but feel that this entire conversation could wait until they had all returned to the castle.

"Come, Neale," Sir Garrick continued, as though reading Reeve's thoughts. "This is no place for this discussion. Why did you not simply ride into Rennart

Castle with your father?" Sir Garrick was now sliding from his horse, hand on his sword.

Gulping, Reeve followed the knight down to the road, despite having no weapon of his own. The rain was now subsiding as quickly as it had begun.

"My father thought it better not to alert Airl Buckthorn to my visit home," Neale said. "It is much easier to take a man by surprise from within his own walls, don't you think? He bides his time, pretending to be concerned about his missing son, drinking with your Airl, the traitor."

Sir Garrick's pace slowed, but his voice remained level. "I see," he said. "And you, Neale? What have you been doing while your father has been . . . biding? Have you been waiting for me?"

Neale cackled, and the lantern swung. "Don't be ridiculous. I have been spying for King and Cartreff, sire, for it is what I am good at. Not that you would know. You have always underestimated me."

"I see," Sir Garrick said again, but this time he sounded angry.

"Don't you want to know what I've uncovered?" Neale taunted. "Apart from your Airl's treason, which is bad enough. But then there's the fact that you, the great Knight Protector of Rennart Castle, allow a coven of witches to operate under your nose . . . even your closest allies in treason will not stand for that!"

A slight hitch in the sloshing sound that marked Sir Garrick's measured pace was the only hint Reeve had that the knight had hesitated. "Fact? You know naught of what you speak," Sir Garrick said. "There are no witches in Rennart Forest."

Reeve held his tongue, keeping Maven's secret. He believed that she and Myra and the other women were not witches — he'd seen no sign of dark magic in their carved underground hideaway — but he had no doubt that most men, including the Airl and Sir Garrick if it came to it, would not bother to ask more questions if the meeting place was discovered.

And that any suggestion of witchcraft in Rennart would see Airl Buckthorn ostracized.

"*Ha!*" laughed Neale, the lantern flickering with his derisive mirth. "How little you know, Sir Garrick. I have heard the whispers about that circle of spies in skirts, and I will unearth them."

Reeve took note of "will unearth" and breathed a sigh of relief, knowing that if Neale had found any true evidence he would have thrown it in Sir Garrick's face. The knight also seemed to relax.

"Whispers," Sir Garrick said. "You skulk about out here in the rain on the strength of whispers? Neale, have I taught you nothing?"

The faint amusement in Sir Garrick's voice seemed to incite Neale to madness, and Reeve remembered, too late, the Cook's words about his terrible temper. "They meet in your very own forest, and you know nothing about it," Neale shouted. "I have but one more stop to prove it and then I will join my father at Rennart Castle in the King's name. We will destroy your Airl, those women – and you. You will not stop us now!"

At the last word, Neale thrust the bright lantern toward Sir Garrick's face, blinding him, before tossing it into the brambles on the roadside, plunging them all into darkness. Even as Reeve ran toward Sir Garrick, he heard a scuffle and then a cry, followed by a thud and running footsteps.

"A knife," Sir Garrick croaked. "He's got a knife . . ."

Reaching his master, Reeve dropped to his knees, peering into the darkness. "I am cut," Sir Garrick said, reaching for Reeve's hand and pressing it into his own side. "The darkness was his cover, and I am wounded."

Reeve swallowed hard in a suddenly dry mouth as he felt the warm, thick, viscous blood seeping through Sir Garrick's tunic. Reeve felt his head begin to swim, and blinked hard to clear his vision.

I cannot see the blood, Reeve reminded himself. How he wished he'd remembered to get that tincture from Myra, but he'd been so distracted by the death of Sully and by Maven and her tales of secret societies that he'd clean forgotten about it.

"Wait here," Reeve said out loud to Sir Garrick. "I'll grab my saddlecloth to bind it." He rushed away, more than happy to take a moment to steady his queasiness.

It took only a few moments to unbuckle his saddle, remove the blue cloth beneath it and tighten the girth again.

Reeve had just stepped back from the horse when lightning cleaved the night sky with a crackle, and the horse danced sideways.

"Whoa there," Reeve said, reaching for her reins, but he was too late. As thunder boomed, the horse took flight, mane standing on end, ears pressed forward, head down as she galloped off into the night. With a shrill neigh, the knight's charger took off at the mare's heels, the drumming of hooves providing a rhythmic counterpoint to the fading roll of the thunder.

Watching them go, Reeve wiped his mud-spattered face as his heart sank. The rain had become a soft drizzle, but that was the only high point he could see as he dropped to Sir Garrick's side and pressed the sodden saddlecloth against his side.

"It seems we are in trouble, young squire," said Sir Garrick, and Reeve caught the brief flash of his grin in the darkness. "We must get to the castle — if Lord Mallor remains inside the walls, our Airl is in danger."

"Can you stand, sire?" Reeve asked, his thoughts buzzing.

"I'm game if you are," the knight answered, and Reeve could almost hear him gritting his teeth.

"If you hold the blanket, I'll help you," Reeve said, moving behind Sir Garrick so that he could support his back as the man sat up.

"Ooooh," Sir Garrick murmured, drawing a long, deep breath.

Reeve waited a moment. "We need to get you to the castle, sire," he said evenly, pushing down the fear rising in his throat. "But first we must get you to your feet."

"Each goal seems as far as the other right now," Sir Garrick muttered.

"One step at a time, sire," said Reeve, forcing heartiness into his voice. Reeve was well aware that he was the only thing standing between a long, slow, liquid death on the side of this road for Sir Garrick and the safety of the castle.

As long as Reeve didn't think too much about that liquid, seeping in waves from Sir Garrick's side, he would be fine. He hoped.

Hauling his master to his feet with as much delicacy as he could manage, Reeve ignored the oaths Sir Garrick whispered and concentrated instead on mustering up every encouraging word he'd ever learned and delivering them in that same bright, breezy tone.

"It's no use," Sir Garrick said a few minutes later, sagging to his knees. "I have the strength of a kitten.

I cannot go on. You go, Reeve – go and fetch help. Tell the Airl everything. We must get word to him that the castle is under siege from within – and we must get there before Neale finishes his mysterious 'one more stop.'"

Reeve looked down at Sir Garrick, feeling helpless. "I can't leave you here in the dark and the rain. You might die before I return. And that's not even considering if Neale comes back."

"I will most certainly die if you don't go now," Sir Garrick said with a harsh laugh. He lay down on the side of the road. "And the Airl may very well be lost to us, as well. Go now!"

Reeve frantically tried to calculate the distance to the castle. He could now see the lights shining, like beacons through the light rain, at the top of the hill, but Reeve figured that he was still a good mile or two from the gates.

He might, Reeve thought, be somewhere near the incredible underground lair of the Beech Circle, but Reeve knew he'd never find it through the trees in the dark. Then there was the fact that, while Sir Garrick might survive if Reeve was to take him there, Reeve himself would surely die a torturous death overseen by Maven herself for exposing the Circle's secret meeting place.

What to do? He remembered that he'd been on his way to see Myra when he'd come across Sully, and that he'd been sent in this direction to find her – so did that mean her hut was nearby?

"Sire," he said, "cover your ears."

"My what?" Sir Garrick snorted, weakly. "If my ears have survived this ridiculous thunder, they will survive whatever you do next. Besides, if I cover my ears, I'll likely bleed to death, Reeve, given one of my hands is busy being soaked with blood through this cloth I'm holding. Just get on with it."

With that, he was silent, and Reeve cupped his hands around his mouth, took a huge breath and shouted: "MYRA!"

He stopped, waiting, but all he could hear was the soft drip of rain on the brambles that lined the road.

Reeve took another deep breath and tried again: "*Myra!*"

Again, he paused, listening hard, but heard no answering shout. Reeve bit his lip. Could it be that he was wrong and his sense of direction was more befuddled by the dark and the rain than he'd thought? Was he as crazy as Neale seemed to be to imagine that he could just conjure up help with a shout?

"*Myra!*" he screamed.

"Who is it that you call for?" Sir Garrick asked hoarsely.

"The wyld woman," Reeve said.

Sir Garrick groaned. "She will not answer you. Her kind does not seek the company of knights and squires."

Reeve bit his lip as Sir Garrick moaned. Still, there

was no movement in the trees, no light, no answering call. It seemed that either the knight was right and Myra would not answer, or Reeve was wrong in thinking her hut was nearby. Either way, Reeve was alone with this problem, and he needed to work out what he was going to do.

"Sir Garrick is right," he said out loud to bolster his own spirits, hoping that Sir Garrick was now too far steeped in pain to listen to him. "Myra does not have to run to the aid of any squire who calls her name."

"It is true," came a laughing voice from behind Reeve, "that I would not choose to ask you and Sir Garrick for dinner, but given the volume of your desperate shouting, I suspect it's not dinner that you are after."

Reeve whirled around, relief flooding through his entire body, to face Myra — and Maven.

"What are you doing here?" he sputtered, surprise making him rude.

"Lady Cassandra sent me to see Myra," Maven responded, with a quick glance toward Sir Garrick. "And it is lucky for you that she did. Myra was walking me back to the castle after the rain when we heard your shout. Otherwise, you would still be shouting!"

"How now, young Reeve," Myra said as Maven lifted the lantern she held to light the scene. Unlike Neale, she was careful to hold it so that it illuminated the road without blinding Reeve. "What seems to be the trouble?"

"I am bleeding," Sir Garrick moaned.

Reeve did not miss the sharp glance that Myra shot his way, and knew she was wondering how Reeve was coping with the blood. He managed a weak smile, making another mental note to ask her for that tincture, and she said nothing, moving around Reeve to kneel beside Sir Garrick.

"You have done well to stem the bleeding with this cloth," Myra said.

Reeve basked a little in her praise, even as her words conjured up that image of the blood seeping from Sir Garrick's wound. Feeling light-headed, all he could do was nod in response.

Myra stood and turned to Maven. "We will need to get him to my hut immediately. I have herbs that will help to stem the flow of blood, and we can clean the wound and stitch it back together."

Reeve grimaced, hoping he wouldn't be required to participate in any stitching, but Maven simply nodded as though what was happening was an everyday occurrence. She really was the most annoyingly unflappable girl he'd ever met.

"Who did this thing?" Myra asked Sir Garrick as Maven moved to the knight's other side and helped the wyld woman to lift him to his feet.

"It was Neale," Reeve responded, unable to keep

the surprise he continued to feel from his voice, as Sir Garrick let out a long moan.

"Neale," breathed Maven, as though the answer was confirmation to a question he had not asked. Reeve waited, but Maven said no more, and he could almost hear her mind ticking over in the dark.

Myra glanced at her but directed her question to Reeve. "I thought Neale had disappeared," she said.

"He had," Reeve said. "But it seems he only went home to bring his father into Rennart Castle to accuse the Airl of treason."

Sir Garrick coughed. "And of harboring witches," he muttered.

Once again, Reeve caught the glance between Myra and Maven. "Witches?" Myra laughed. "Well now, Sir Garrick, you know that the only wyld woman around here is me, and if I were able to summon spells I'd have taken myself off to better circumstances years ago."

"That's what I told him," Sir Garrick said. "But he was quite certain there's a network of witches – spies in skirts, he called them – working against the King here in Rennart Forest. Need to warn the Airl about that – the slightest hint of it will have his friends and allies turning on him."

"We need to warn the Airl about a few things, I think,"

said Maven quickly. "I'll go to see him now. Here, Reeve, take my place."

Before he'd had a chance to think, Reeve found himself tucked under Sir Garrick's arm, staggering under his weight while Maven disappeared back through the trees the way she and Myra had come.

"Treason and witches and spies, was it?" asked Myra, drawing Sir Garrick's attention away from Maven. "Quite the list. Next thing, he'll be accusing the Airl of taking the Fire Star as well."

"Only thing Neale didn't mention," Sir Garrick said with a laugh that ended in a wretched cough. "Can't help but think he probably stole it himself."

Suddenly, a dark shape snaked through the trees, erupting into a volley of snarls and barks at Reeve's feet.

"Blast!" said Sir Garrick, echoing Reeve's thoughts.

"Down, Baron," snapped Myra, and the dog subsided immediately, moving to Myra's side with a whimper of greeting.

"Good boy," she murmured. "These are friends."

With his heart beating fast from the scare, Reeve saw with relief the shadowy outline of a cottage before them, camouflaged by tree trunks, no hint of light to be seen. He heard the soft clucking of chickens, but could see no pen.

"You're lucky I've put the geese to bed," Myra said, as she and Reeve lowered Sir Garrick to a sitting position on the edge of the porch. "If Baron gives you a fright in the dark, you don't want to come across a pack of hissing, snapping geese."

"I'll take your word for it," said Sir Garrick, lying down on the wooden boards as Myra moved to open the front door. Soon, a warm glow of light issued from inside the hut, and Reeve could see that, though built from rough-hewn wood, it was snug and watertight.

"Boots and cloak off," Myra ordered.

Reeve placed the sword on the porch as he bent to help Sir Garrick ease his boots from his feet and unfasten the wet cloak that covered him. With this done, Myra helped Reeve to once again get Sir Garrick to his feet and, after Reeve had removed his own cloak and toed off his boots, over the threshold and onto the narrow bed tucked against the far wall of the hut's living space.

In the light, Reeve could see that the saddle blanket was now bright red with blood, and he backed away as swiftly as he could, blinking furiously at a room that was suddenly swimming.

"Right," said Myra, drawing his attention, "Reeve, you go outside to the well and fetch me a fresh bucket of water. The bucket's just outside the door, well's out the back." Without waiting for a response, she turned back to the bed and began lifting the knight's tunic.

Grateful for the respite, Reeve turned and fled the room, pulling the door behind him as he took deep breaths of the still-moist night air. The rain had finally stopped, so he left his cloak hanging by the door, pulling on his boots and picking up the wooden pail. As Reeve stepped down from the porch and made his way around the building, he could hear the steady dripping of water as it worked its way down through the dense branches of the trees around him.

A fat drop of rain hit the back of his neck, and he shivered.

It was so quiet, Reeve could hear the soft squelch of his waterlogged boots and the suck of mud underfoot with each step. By the time he reached the back of the cottage, the moon was peeking out from behind the dark clouds overhead, but the light came and went as the clouds scudded past, blown by some wind on high.

Reeve was able to pick out a snug little henhouse, surrounded by a fence of woven twigs. Set high on poles to the right of the enclosure, a ramp led up to the henhouse's firmly closed door. Reeve could not help but creep up to peek over the fence, hoping for a glimpse of the aforementioned geese, but could not see so much as a feather.

Another fence of woven twigs wrapped around the poles under the henhouse, and he could only imagine that Myra had shut the geese in there.

A scuttling noise in the forest beyond had Reeve stepping back, shifting the pail to his left hand. "Who's there?" he called, hating the thin, high voice that emerged as his nerves took over.

The only response was a wave of outraged clucking from the henhouse, which was all but drowned out by the aggressive honking from the enclosed area beneath it.

"Okay, okay," Reeve said, backing away from the outside fence. "I'm going."

The clouds parted overhead, and moonlight poured through the gap, allowing Reeve to see the well on the opposite side of the clearing. Reeve crossed to it and lowered the bucket down on its sturdy rope until it hit the water below with a splash. He grasped the rope and began to haul the bucket back up, hand over hand, trying to keep it from hitting the side of the well and spilling its precious cargo.

Reeve had just caught a glimpse of the top of the bucket, the water reflecting in the moonlight, when the chickens and geese erupted again, giving him such a fright that he almost dropped the rope. Twisting to see behind him without letting go of the bucket, Reeve scanned the area but could see nothing.

"What is it?" he called to the restless birds, receiving no answer. He was about to turn back to his task, discounting the disturbance as a fox that had wandered too close, when a black shadow hurtled from the tree line, barking and snapping.

This time, Reeve did drop the bucket, ready to run for the safety of the cottage lest Baron turn on him, but it took Reeve only a moment to realize that the dog's attention was not on him. Reeve froze as the frenzy of howls and growls rose from the other side of the cottage, a panicked shout rising above the noise.

Then Reeve heard the terrible shriek of a dog in pain, and he forgot to be frightened as he realized that Myra's pet had been hurt. Running toward the sound, he rounded the corner of the cottage and almost fell over Baron, whimpering in the mud. There was no sign of whoever had been shouting.

"It's okay, boy," Reeve said, crouching down beside the dog and reaching out a tentative hand to stroke one ear. "You'll be okay."

He ran his hand over the animal, who seemed too hurt or shocked to react, and gasped when he felt a sticky patch on Baron's belly, grateful that the force of his anger seemed to offset the lurch of his stomach.

"Who did this to you?" he asked out loud, reaching under Baron with both hands and staggering to his feet with the whining dog in his arms.

"I did!" came a loud voice behind him, and Reeve turned to face Neale of Broadfield, still brandishing his long knife. "That's her familiar, you know, the wyld woman's. She uses that beast in black magic."

Reeve snuggled Baron closer to his chest. "He's a dog," he said evenly, trying to ignore the feeling of spreading moisture across his already wet tunic. He couldn't afford to think about the fact that the dog was bleeding all over him. Not now.

"He's a dog," Reeve repeated, playing for time. "And Myra is no witch." Reeve didn't know much about witches, but if there was any magic at all in her, surely she wouldn't be living in a tiny cottage in the woods? If Reeve could conjure up anything he wanted, it wouldn't be this . . .

"You know nothing," Neale sneered. "Look at you. You weren't good enough to squire for Sir Garrick two years ago and you're still not. But no matter. Once the King hears of the Airl's treason — and he soon will hear — the Airl and all at Rennart Castle will hang. Those who last that long!"

The moon spilled through a gap in the clouds and Reeve could see Neale's face, twisted with anger and hatred as he waved his bloody knife above his head. Any thoughts Reeve had of trying to talk to Neale, to make him see reason, disappeared and, without another word, Reeve turned and fled toward the henhouse, stumbling a little under Baron's weight. His only thought was to get inside the hen enclosure and put a fence between himself and Neale.

Panting, Reeve slithered and slipped through the mud, Neale right behind him. Reeve reached the gate, fumbling for the catch, Baron whining in pain as his hind legs slipped from Reeve's grasp. Gathering up the dog, Reeve slid through the gate with barely enough time to shove it closed with his hip and lean against it, grateful for Baron's extra weight to help him hold back the assault from the enraged Neale on the other side.

With the gate shifting and bucking behind him, the geese honking and hissing, the hens squawking and clucking, and Baron whimpering in his arms, Reeve tried to calm his breathing. He knew that the calmest mind always won a battle, but his training had not prepared him for the rattling of his heart, the rolling of his stomach and the twitching of his limbs when under true threat.

There was no escape from the noisy enclosure, and he wasn't going to be able to keep Neale out much longer. He wanted to shout, but Sir Garrick was no use to him and he didn't want Myra facing this crazed version of Neale.

"Let the geese out."

Reeve started at the slurred voice from the other side of the dark enclosure, barely heard above the cacophony. Squinting, he could just make out a figure, slumped on the ground against the fence, a cider bottle within reach.

"Kit?" Reeve whispered in amazement. "Is that you?"

"Actually," Kit went on as though Reeve hadn't spoken, perhaps because he hadn't heard him, "probably best if you stay there for a minute. I'll do it."

Reeve could only watch, his full body weight leaning against the gate that banged and clattered behind him, as Kit dragged himself slowly to his feet and ambled across the enclosure toward the geese pen beneath the henhouse.

"Right-ho," Kit shouted a moment later. "When I say go, get out of the way."

"But —"

"Go!" Kit said, and opened the pen, unleashing an angry mass of spitting, hissing, clattering white birds. For a moment, Reeve froze, then realized they were heading straight for him — and they were enormous!

Jumping away from the gate, Baron heavy in his arms, Reeve took one big step to the side. The gate flew open and Neale tumbled through, landing in a heap in the mud as he lashed right and left with his knife. Within seconds, the geese were upon him, running over the top of him in their single-minded drive to get out through the gate.

Reeve watched open-mouthed as Neale tried to fight the geese off, merely inciting them to further rage. As Neale tried to stagger to his feet, the geese attacked, flying at him until he threw himself to the ground once more, trying to protect his head from the furious beaks.

"C'mon!" Kit was standing beside Reeve, the ever-present jug of cider now in one hand. "They'll turn on us next."

"We can't just leave him here!" Reeve shouted. "They'll kill him!"

Kit bent down and picked up the knife that Neale had lost in the geese's initial attack. "No more than he deserves?" He dangled the blade between his fingers so that it glinted in the moonlight.

Reeve took in the figure struggling on the ground, feathers flying around him. Then Baron whimpered in his arms, and he remembered Neale's cruelty.

"Let's get Myra," Reeve said. "She'll be able to corral the geese again."

"Sure," Kit said. "Let's do that. But maybe we'll walk very slowly . . ."

With that, he led the way to the gate and Reeve followed, ignoring Neale's shouts behind him. He'd never actually heard of anyone being pecked to death by geese, so he thought Neale was probably safe enough really. But the birds would keep Neale in one place until Reeve and Sir Garrick worked out what to do with him and that, thought Reeve, wasn't a bad thing.

As they left the enclosure, Kit pulled the gate shut behind Reeve, dropping the latch back into place.

"Better safe than sorry," Kit said with a wink.

Reeve couldn't help but agree.

CHAPTER TWENTY

I am breaking every rule in the servant handbook by entering the castle keep by the main steps, but it is, strangely, the only way for me to enter unseen. If I were to go via the kitchen, I would be recognized in an instant and word of my presence would travel the halls ahead of me. But this way . . .

At least it has stopped raining. I take a moment to stop by the water barrel in the main square, using the light from a smoking, recently relit torch nearby to check my appearance. There is not much I can do about my sodden cloak, so I remove it and shove it behind the barrel before quickly rebraiding my damp hair, smoothing it behind my ears, and do my best to pull the worst wrinkles from my serviceable gown.

As I approach the sentry and reach the bottom of the steep stone steps that lead to the imposing, arched doorway, I channel my mother, standing straight and imperious, my face a haughty mask. My gown may be plain brown, but a trained servant will still note the fineness of the cloth, the quality of the trim. Assuming, that is, that the sentry can see anything beyond my face in the torchlight.

Fortunately, the gown is long enough to hide the mud-stained boots beneath.

Without acknowledging the sentry, I sweep past him, focusing on the door, subtly kicking each step with the toe of my boot so that I may glide toward the top without ever looking down. I have never been so glad of my mother's insistence on deportment lessons. Hours and hours spent walking around with a book on my head for this one moment.

"Oi!" For the barest moment, I freeze at the sentry's voice but force myself forward. No lady would allow herself to be spoken to thus, and a lady I must be right now.

"Oi!" the oaf repeats, and this time I allow myself to turn on my heel. He is staring up at me from the bottom step, squinting in the dim light.

"Surely you do not address me?" I say, mimicking Mama's iciest tone. "One such as you would not say 'oi' to Lady Maven of Aramoor, here for the wedding on the morrow?"

"I'm —" He pauses a moment, and I hold my breath as he seems to deliberate, his gaze taking in my appearance from my shoes to my set, stony face.

"Sorry, my lady," he says after a long pause. "I was addressing a rogue on the steps behind you."

I wait a beat to let him know that I do not believe a word and then incline my head majestically, letting him off the hook. As he turns back to his position with relief, I continue toward the doors, fighting the urge to run as fast as I can to my lady and thence to warn the Airl of the danger beneath his roof.

I do not know what Neale knows, or thinks he knows, of Airl Buckthorn's feelings toward the King, but I do know that Lord Mallor must be removed from the castle immediately, lest we all be in terrible danger. Given the two men are equals in social standing, it must be handled with great care, lest we spark a civil war. I have no idea of Airl Buckthorn's plans, but my father's teachings on war strategy have shown me that war is never a good idea — and a war on your doorstep when you are unprepared for it is the very worst idea of all.

As I reach the top step, unseen hands draw the doors inward, and I continue to glide past the footmen, keeping my head down. It is only when I reach the end of the grand hallway, with its flagstone floor and soaring wood-paneled walls, that I lift my skirts and begin to run.

I can only pray Cassandra is still in her rooms.

Ribald male laughter slides out from under the door to the Airl's solar, filling the air around us with its harsh, knowing sound, and I feel Cassandra quail. From the moment that I burst into her bedchamber, quickly filling her in on all that had passed as I laced her into her emerald-green gown, she has been with me. But now, at the last hurdle, she falters.

"You must, my lady," I say. "I cannot do this. It must be you."

Still she hesitates.

"Sir Garrick is hurt," I repeat. "The Airl will want to know that — and he *must* know the rest."

Cassandra reaches out a shaking hand to the door handle. I understand her fear — the world of men is foreign to her, and barging into this room will bring all male eyes upon her, with no support bar an uncle who is not best pleased with her as it is. This holds not the fun and pageantry of her first night in the Great Hall, when hundreds of eyes — men, women and children — played witness; this is menacing and serious.

"Sir Garrick needs you," I say. "The Airl needs you. The Circle needs you. Please, Cassandra. Just tell him you must speak to him out here, and I'll do the rest."

Perhaps it is because I, always so very careful to maintain my servant's position, refer to her as an equal, that she lifts her chin, and turns the handle. As she steps through the door, all sound from within ceases, as though a thick quilt has been thrown over the room.

"What is the meaning of this?" I hear the Airl roar as the door closes, and the tone is enough to make me tremble, even through the thick wood.

I wait, pacing upon the stones for endless moments as the clock in the hall ticks. I'd told Lady Cassandra that she cannot mention Sir Garrick or Neale in front of Lord Mallor but must somehow bring her uncle through the door nonetheless. All the way here, she'd been trying to think of the best way to do so.

Suddenly, the door bangs against the wall as it opens, and the Airl strides into the hallway, fury making his very steps bristle. "Well?" he roars again. "Where is she?"

I stare at Cassandra, who closes the door gently before turning to face her uncle.

"Anice is not here," she says as I silently approve the tack she has taken. "As far as I know, she's safely in her rooms and not, in fact, covered in straw from her roll in the hay with a stable hand."

Even under the circumstances, I can feel my mouth twitch as I try not to laugh.

"You lied to me?" the Airl says, his frown deepening. "And such a lie?"

"The worst of it is that you had no trouble believing me," Cassandra throws at him, hands on her hips and, to his credit, a shadow of shame crosses his features. "But we have no time to debate this now. You must eject Lord Mallor from the castle with haste."

The Airl laughs. "And why would I do such a thing?"

Cassandra turns to me. "Maven will tell you."

As the Airl turns his disbelieving stare upon me, it is my turn to quail, but I force myself not to flinch. This man holds my future in his hands, and one gesture from him will see me in a nunnery – or worse – forevermore. But, I remind myself, he needs what I know. I am safe for the moment.

And so I begin, relaying all I know of Neale and what he has told his father, about the whispers of treason that Lord Mallor is determined to blow into a raging shout that will reach all the way to the King's ears. And if I leave out Neale's comments about "spies in skirts," well, who is to question me right here and now? Not Cassandra, standing silently, wringing her hands, that's for sure.

"Sir Garrick is cared for?" says the Airl as soon as I draw breath, and my estimation of him goes up when his first concern is for his knight.

"In the best hands," I say.

"And you are certain that Neale has told his father his . . . thoughts," the Airl says.

I nod. "He said as much to Sir Garrick and his squire Reeve."

The Airl considers my words. "And Neale is . . . where now?"

"I do not know," I admit. "With Sir Garrick stabbed in the darkness, Reeve was unable to say, only that Neale had run from them."

The Airl stares over my head down the hallway, deep in thought. "But he was on his way here? To his father?"

"So I believe. It was with much relief that I found I had arrived before him."

The Airl pauses a moment and then looks at me. "Are you capable of some mummery, girl?"

I frown. "Playacting?" I pretend to consider, though the truth is that I have been acting a role my entire life and am acting one right now. "I'm sure I could manage something. What is it you wish me to do?"

The Airl's smile is cold. "I will return to my solar. You will hear laughter as I make light of Cassandra's intrusion, and then I want you to run in, as though just from outdoors, and tell everything you know of Neale's whereabouts."

I see his plan immediately. Lord Mallor is a danger

inside the castle, but he would be more dangerous if the Airl attempts to remove him by force. Better to send him out into the darkness with his entourage on the word of a sighting of his "disappeared" son, and then bar the gates against his return.

"Not everything," I say.

The Airl gives me an approving nod. "You catch on quickly, girl," he says. "Enough that Airl Broadfield cannot avoid leaving Rennart Castle lest he appear uncaring. Not enough for him to know that we wish to remove him."

He places one hand on the doorknob. "Oh, and don't mention Sir Garrick," he says, his face set in hard lines. "We shall keep that information for the right moment."

The door closes, and Cassandra takes my hand. "You play a dangerous game now," she says.

I laugh. "It has always been dangerous. But better, don't you think, than embroidery or pianoforte practice?"

Cassandra grins – her hatred of both these things is a long-standing joke between us. "Indeed. I will wait in my rooms to hear from you."

Before she leaves, she removes the locket from her neck, clasping it around mine. I do not need to open it to see the tiny painting – the Beech Circle is with me.

"Go well," she says before hurrying away, head down.

I wait in silence until I hear a roar of hearty guffaws

from within. Hitching my skirts so that now my mud-stained boots can be seen, I quickly muss my hair before banging on the door.

"Enter!" comes the Airl's command.

Taking a deep breath, I push the door open, well aware that it is down to me to deliver just the right amount of detail to remove the enemy within like a canker.

"My lord!" I say, keeping my eyes on him and allowing my voice to tremble.

And I begin.

The shouting and clattering from the courtyard still seems to ring through the castle. Having delivered my message to the Airl and been summarily dismissed, I take my time wending my way back through the hallways toward Cassandra's rooms. There is no more I can do for now, and so I must wait.

She is not here and her outdoor boots are missing, so I assume that she has gone to watch the spectacle of Lord Mallor's departure with the Airl. It is not until I stretch across the bottom of the feather mattress that I realize how tired I am, and yet my mind whirls with all that has happened this night.

Lord Mallor's response to my story of Neale wandering alone and helpless in the forest, badly affected by a mania surely brought on by an animal bite, had been fascinating to watch. On one hand, he'd known that Neale had been fine mere hours before – known it because he had himself been with Neale. On the other, however, he could not ignore the news – not only because to do so would make him look uncaring in front of his peers, but because he couldn't discount the possibility that my story was true, and that something had happened to Neale after Lord Mallor had left him.

It was all Airl Buckthorn could do to suppress his glee as, after a brief pause, Neale's father had announced he would ride for the forest immediately, taking one of his men to help search.

Airl Buckthorn had responded swiftly, insisting on accompanying Lord Mallor and suggesting that, given the size of Rennart Forest, he would need all five of his men to help with the search.

"In fact," Airl Buckthorn had finished, "I'll bring six of my own knights along . . . just to ensure everything goes well."

And so, Lord Mallor and his men had been ejected from within the castle walls, his wedding invitation revoked, with nary a drop of blood spilled nor an accusation of treason voiced. The Airl would diplomatically ensure he did not return, and he could take his unhappiness and his unfounded accusations to the King – at least two days' ride away – if he had a problem with that.

I would be congratulating myself on an excellent night's work were it not for the fact that Sir Garrick is injured, Neale still unaccounted for, Sully's murderer still on the loose and the Fire Star still missing.

It is this thought that has me back on my feet, pacing.

I confess that, for a brief moment, in the very first instance, I had wondered if the thief had been Neale, who, as Sir Garrick's squire, had always enjoyed free run of the castle and would understand the best places to stash the stone. The fact that he'd disappeared had also counted against him.

But I had discounted him quickly. And, from what Reeve said, I was right to do so. The timing was all wrong for starters, and Reeve reported that his ravings were centered on the King and the Beech Circle, in spirit if not in name. No mention of the Fire Star.

Which means, as I suspected, that Sully's murderer, and the potential possessor of the stone, is closer to home.

I pause. There is still no sign of Cassandra, and I know that she will not stop me in my search for the Fire Star. Why should I wait for her now?

Before the thought is even complete, I am back in the halls of the castle, following the torches as I make my way back toward the ground floor, deep in thought as I consider and discard first one suspect and then another.

Until I am circling back to one thought over and over. *Someone saw.*

"Where go you, Maven?"

The frosty voice of Lorimer drags me from my thoughts, and I bristle at the interrogative tone.

"I go to my lady," I say, before allowing myself, just this once, to snap back. "Not that it is any of your business."

Lorimer takes a step closer, and his sneer is clear in the lamplight. "Everything in this castle is my business," he says. "It would do you well to remember that. You are not who you once were, girl, and you answer to me now."

I want to step back, away from his looming presence and the faint, sour smell of ale on his breath, but I do not. Instead, I draw once again on years of Mama's training to instill as much insolence as I can into my blank face.

"I see," I say, keeping my tone measured. "And yet I am not of this castle. Not yet. As a visitor to Rennart, I answer to my Lady Cassandra and to no one else."

He says nothing for a long moment. "Very well, but I would speak with you. It is about the wedding tomorrow."

I am wary, but I remember looking down from my lady's rooms and wondering about the view from Lorimer's lair. This is one way to get inside again to take note of exactly what can be seen from there.

"Very well," I say, echoing his tone, "but my lady is expecting me, so we must be brief."

I follow him along the hallway, down the stairs, past the kitchen and into his parlor, realizing as I enter that we have seen no one along the way. Even the kitchen is silent, as though every inhabitant of the castle went out to the courtyard to watch Lord Mallor depart.

The air in Lorimer's room is stuffy as he takes his seat behind his desk, leaving me to stand, like a naughty child, on the rug before him. I look around the room, trying to make it seem as though I'm interested in his trove of secondhand treasures.

When my glance reaches the window, however, I have to suppress a groan. I can see nothing but my own face reflected back at me and a halo of light beyond. It is too dark in this corner of the courtyard, bar one solitary lamp, to get a sense of the view.

I will need to press my nose to the glass to see if my instincts are correct.

"What is it you wish to discuss with me?" I prompt, trying to think how I can unobtrusively sidle over to the window.

Lorimer picks up a quill, tapping it against his fingers as he considers me. His chair creaks beneath him, and I can hear the ticking of the large wooden clock hanging just beside the door. It occurs to me how very thick the stone walls are down here.

"I know what you did," Lorimer says, placing the quill on the desk before him and lacing his fingers together.

My thoughts begin to buzz, remembering Lorimer's web of informants within these walls. But I hold my expression still. "I have no idea what you're talking about," I say, looking over his head once again at the painting.

Lorimer jumps to his feet and moves around the desk to grab my arm. "I know what you did. I know what you had planned."

"Unhand me, steward!" I say, keeping my voice even. "You have no rights over my person. My Lady Cassandra will not be pleased that you are manhandling her companion."

"Bah!" Lorimer says, his face twisted with derision. "Companion! You are a servant, girl, just like me. No better. Not anymore."

"No," I say, and I pull out my haughtiest tone. "You saw to that."

"Ha!" he laughs. "Your father was ready enough to do that all by himself."

"By himself? I think not. Who was it that hid his debts until they consumed him? Who was it that ensured he got to those games on time? Why, his faithful steward, of course. His faithful steward who had his own gambling problem. Does the Airl know?"

Lorimer freezes at my question. "You don't know what you're talking about."

I turn my head to look at him. "Don't I? I may have been a child, but I was the only one in the household who put two and two together."

Lorimer pauses. "You've heard too many fairy tales. You're making it up . . ."

I can almost hear Lorimer's mind working. "There's no proof of that," he continues, sounding surer. "No one would ever believe such a thing."

The words Lorimer speaks so closely echo those of my mother that I have to close my eyes. At ten years of age, I had begged and pleaded with her to listen to me, but now, five years later and much wiser in the ways of the world, I say nothing. He is right. No one will ever believe me. Not even my own mother.

"You can never prove it, girl," Lorimer repeats, and now he is exultant in the way that only a scoundrel can be when he's gotten away with his con.

"I cannot," I concede, unable to look at him. "But I know it's true."

"You always were too clever for your own good," Lorimer snarls. I look into his twisted face and see no sign of the smooth servant. "But, so help me, you will learn your place. As will that harlot Cassandra. Now, give me the Fire Star."

Even as he grabs both my arms, hard, twisting them together as he pulls me toward him, my mind is turning over. Lorimer knows about our plans but does not have the stone! My instincts were correct: someone saw — Lorimer saw — but Sully did not have the Fire Star on his person when he was left on the side of the road!

But there is no time to think of this now, with Lorimer's fingers bruising my skin, and his grasp on my wrists ensuring I cannot dig into my pocket for my knife.

This is the man beneath the bland face of the superior servant, and he is without reason or thought. I pull hard, but I cannot loosen his grip, so I clench my hands and strike up hard with both arms, driving my fists under his chin. He swears as he reels back, letting go of me.

Even as I duck away, however, he is raising his hand and I am not quick enough. He catches the side of my head with his fist, leaving my ears ringing and my balance swirling.

"*I don't have it!*" I shout, shaking my head, stumbling backward as I try to clear the fog that blurs my vision, fumbling for the knife in the hidden pocket in my skirt. And then he raises his fist again, and the world goes black.

His voice comes into focus first.

"Wake up, you silly girl," Lorimer says, patting

me roughly on the cheek. "Wake up! I didn't hit you that hard."

I groan as I haul myself to a sitting position. How long have I been lying here? Long enough to feel stiff and sore.

"You should not have hit me at all," I say, and my voice sounds muffled to my own ears.

In answer, Lorimer grabs hold of my hair and yanks upward, giving me no choice but to scramble to my feet. As I do so, he grasps each hand, pulling them together behind my back before holding both my wrists securely in one hand.

"You know where it is! He gave it back to you," Lorimer snarls, and I feel his other hand pull on my braid, wrenching my head back so hard I cannot look anywhere but upward — and cannot fight him. "I know he did. I need that stone."

He. Sully. I no longer need to press my face to any window to confirm that it was Lorimer who saw Sully catch the stone. And I do not need him to tell me that he followed Sully and killed him. Or why.

"You have debts," I say faintly, feeling sick from the pressure on my neck. Still holding both my wrists in one hand, he bends my elbows, forcing my hands upward between my shoulder blades.

"Not for long," Lorimer says. "I'll take the stone,

pay them off and disappear to Talleben with no one any the wiser."

As he speaks, I can feel him wrapping my braid over my hands, tighter and tighter, contorting me into a painfully restricted position. I cannot lift my head, I cannot lower my hands, and my neck and shoulders are screaming in agony.

A sick sensation floods my stomach. He has killed a man for the stone and will not hesitate to kill me, as well.

"You killed Sully," I croak, stalling for time as I try to think through an escape route. But I can barely breathe and I am so very tired. Surely, someone must come back to the kitchens soon?

"Was that his name?" Lorimer asks, sounding bored as he pulls the end of my braid harder and begins to drag me toward the window. "Your tame servant? What a buffoon. To have the most precious stone in the kingdom in his hands and then to simply hand it back like a lamb. I know you have it, because he did not."

Oh, Sully. Poor, loyal man.

"How do you know he did not sell it himself?" I rasp, wanting desperately to kick out at him or . . . something. But I cannot. My neck is aching and my chin stretched at such an unnatural angle that I must breathe shallow and fast while my chest screams for air and my arms cramp in their uncomfortable position.

Lorimer jerks my braid, pulling me even further backward, and I watch from the corner of my eye as he takes the tasseled cord from the curtains with his free hand, trying to form a loop, and I realize he is going to put that cord around my neck.

I fight my horror as I grasp the fact that this is my chance. My one chance.

Even if he can loop the cord over my head, he will not be able to keep hold of my hair and my hands and pull it tight at the same time.

I force myself to stay calm, but I keep moving my feet, trying to cheat him of a still target for his wicked noose.

"Because it has not turned up in any of the usual places," Lorimer says casually, reminding me that I had asked a question about the Fire Star's whereabouts, something that seems so unimportant to me right at this moment as I feel Lorimer fumbling about, trying to tie the cord around my neck, slowly coming to the same conclusion about my hair as I did. "I checked after I . . . followed him."

As Lorimer says the last words, he releases my braid and my hands in order to drop his noose around my neck. The split second is enough.

With my head spinning and little feeling in the hands still tied up behind my back, I spin around, raising my knee as I do so, barely aware that the parlor's door has crashed open against the wall. With little to guide me but instinct, I drive my knee upward with all of my might.

Lorimer groans, dropping to the floor like a dead weight, landing at my feet as, fighting the pain from cramped arms and the lack of feeling in my fingers, I disentangle my hands from the knot of my braid and reach into my pocket for my knife.

As Lorimer rolls in agony across the green rug, the curtain cord still grasped in one of his hands, I press my foot across his neck and hold the knife above him.

"Don't move," I gasp, though the room still spins and my shoulders pain me. "Not so much as a hair."

"Maven!" I can barely hear Reeve's voice above the roar of sound in my own head as I try to slow my breathing. "Maven, are you all right?"

With one last sharp exhalation to bring myself back under control, I manage to turn toward Reeve, careful not to move my foot.

"I am," I say. "But also glad to see you."

Reeve looks at the man on the floor. "You seem to have everything under control."

And I laugh. And laugh. Like a lunatic.

Like someone who knows she has cheated death.

CHAPTER TWENTY-ONE

Saturday

Spies in skirts. Reeve could not help but recall Neale's words as he watched the Lady Cassandra enter the Great Hall, a vision in cream velvet, her long dark hair lying in curls across her shoulders like a cape. Around her neck, where the Fire Star should have sparkled like a glittering heart, she once again wore her simple silver locket.

A step behind her, protectively hovering even as she marched in time to the music provided by the harpist in the corner, came Maven, her usual simple brown dress discarded in favor of a russet gown that brought a flush to her cheeks.

Or perhaps she was blushing, Reeve thought with a smirk. One as private as Maven would not welcome the eyes of the entire castle community – plus hundreds of guests – upon her.

A gentle nudge brought Reeve's attention back to the man standing beside him. Sir Garrick's face was almost as pale as his bride's cream gown, but he was calm and focused, with none of the unhappy nerves he had displayed only a few days before.

"She is here?" Sir Garrick murmured, facing the clergyman who would perform the marriage service. Custom dictated that the groom not turn his head until the bride was standing beside him, and Sir Garrick would not break protocol, even if he was leaning heavily on a walking stick just to keep himself upright for the service.

"Sire, she is," Reeve answered. He felt, rather than heard, the knight's sigh of relief.

"This pleases you?" Reeve ventured.

Sir Garrick hesitated. "It pleases my Airl Buckthorn," he began, before adding so that only Reeve could hear, "and it pleases me."

Reeve grinned. Negotiations regarding the marriage had continued long into the previous night. The Airl had wanted to hold off, awaiting the return of the Fire Star, his promised dowry. But Sir Garrick had held firm, and Reeve had been impressed by the articulate way the knight had argued his case. It seemed that the Lady Cassandra had made quite an impression on Sir Garrick, and he was determined to have her as his bride.

Eventually, he had played his trump card — if and when the Fire Star did turn up, it was better that Lady Cassandra be safely married into Rennart Castle to ensure there was no question of the stone's ownership. Secretly, Reeve wondered if Sir Garrick had caught wind of Cassandra's plans to flee with the stone, but perhaps he was truly just dedicated to ensuring she become his wife.

Either way, the wedding was upon them, and, within a few short minutes, the Lady Cassandra would wed Sir Garrick, Knight Protector of Rennart Castle.

The sound of giggling from the front row behind him caught Reeve's attention, and he turned slightly. The Lady Anice, resplendent in a bejeweled golden gown that looked gaudy beside the understated elegance of both the bride and her companion, was whispering behind her hand to the girl beside her. As Reeve watched, the two girls turned toward the aisle, making faces at Maven, who glided past as though they did not exist.

Frowning, Reeve shifted his attention to the altar, admiring the way the morning light shone through the red, green and blue panels of the huge stained glass window behind it. The rain of the previous evening was but a memory, and Reeve could hear shouts from the courtyard outside as the castle's servants put the final touches to preparations for the feast that would soon take place.

As soon as Lady Cassandra stepped beside Sir Garrick, the cleric began, rolling through the ceremony in his singsong voice. Reeve tuned out, thinking about the events of the night before. Neale and his father would be almost home to their manor in Broadfield, he supposed, assuming they hadn't stopped to rest en route. Or gone straight to the King.

Neale may have needed a good, long sleep, Reeve conceded, thinking of the last time he'd seen him, staggering toward his father on the road outside Rennart Castle, bruised and battered and covered in geese feathers and worse.

To say that Reeve and Myra had been surprised to meet not only Lord Mallor and his five knights on the road, but the Airl of Buckthorn himself, was an understatement. Reeve suppressed a grin as he thought on the conversation between Myra and Airl Buckthorn.

"We found something you lost, out in the forest," Myra had said, indicating Neale. The former squire was slung between Myra and Reeve, one arm around each, as they'd half carried him from Myra's house to the castle.

"In the forest?" the Airl had responded, looking Neale over, taking in his disheveled state and dazed expression.

"Wandered into my geese pen," Myra had said. "Got himself into a spot of bother."

"Enough, witch!" Lord Mallor had roared. "What have you done to my son?"

Reeve had heard Myra's sharp intake of breath, and had felt the atmosphere around them suddenly become tense.

"Myra saved your son's life," Reeve had said, trying to keep the wobble of nerves from his voice. Lord Mallor was a powerful man, far more so than Reeve's own father, and Reeve had known he was taking a risk in speaking out this way. "As she saved the life of Sir Garrick after your son attacked him! Without her, Airl Buckthorn would have every right to denounce Neale as a murderer."

"Garrick is all right?" the Airl had affirmed while Lord Mallor glowered at Reeve.

"A little weakened by his loss of blood, but well enough to travel by carriage back to his own bed if you'd like to collect him," Myra had responded equably.

With a flick of his head, the Airl had sent one of his own soldiers scrambling back to the castle to fetch transport for the Knight Protector.

"What happened here?" the Airl had asked, at last.

"Let us not discuss this on the road," Lord Mallor had said, dismounting his horse and moving toward his son. "Neale needs attention. We should return to the castle."

Lord Mallor had pushed Reeve aside, putting one arm around Neale's waist, and had taken Reeve's place beneath Neale's left arm.

"I think not," said the Airl with a grim smile. "He may not have succeeded in killing my best knight, but the fact that he tried to do so is enough for me. Neale will not return to Rennart Castle and neither will you."

For a moment, the only sound had been the jingling of horses' bridles as Lord Mallor's men awaited their lord's command. Lord Mallor did not flinch from Airl Buckthorn, who had loomed over him from his horse, soldiers arrayed behind him.

"We have much to speak about," Lord Mallor had ground out, barely moving his lips. "I know what you have done. The King will not be impressed by your lack of hospitality to me and mine."

The Airl had remained stone-faced in the flickering torchlight. "What you think you know is nothing to me," he said. "If the King has problems with my fiefdom, he must come and tell me himself."

Lord Mallor had spat on the road. "You know not what you do."

"I know that I have no time for talking in tongues," the Airl had responded as a cart rumbled down the road behind him. "You, Reeve, take this cart and the wyld woman, and fetch Sir Garrick home."

Then, without awaiting a response from anyone, he'd

turned his horse and galloped away, flicking mud all over a speechless Lord Mallor and his men as he went.

"You will need to get your boy some help," Myra had said, ducking out from under Neale's other arm so that all of the former squire's weight rested upon his father's shoulder. "His mind seems to be wandering."

"You have not heard the last of this," Lord Mallor had shouted as Myra joined Reeve in hopping up on the wooden cart that drew up beside them. "I know all about you and your sorcery. The King will pay me handsomely for the information."

Myra had laughed as the cart began to trundle off down the road toward her cottage. "Pay for the ramblings of a madman?" she'd said. "I think not!"

As the cart had left them behind, however, her face had grown serious. "Did you tell?" she'd whispered to Reeve, and her deep, melodic voice was harsh.

"Me? NO!" Reeve had spluttered. "Neale left the castle before I ever even knew about . . . things. It was not me."

Myra had been silent. "Someone has told. But who?"

To that question, there was no answer, and nothing more to say.

"Reeve?" Sir Garrick nudged him now. "The ring?"

"Oh, wait, what?" Flustered, Reeve fumbled about in his belt before triumphantly producing the ring. Anice's spiteful titter behind him brought a flush of heat to Reeve's face.

"Sorry," he muttered to Sir Garrick, who had turned back to his bride and probably hadn't heard him. Maven clearly had, though, because she sent him a sympathetic glance before turning her head back to the cleric.

Reeve saw the wince of pain that accompanied the movement.

She seemed to have survived her ordeal with Lorimer with just some bruises and stiffness, but Reeve had never been so pleased in his life that, after fetching Sir Garrick and handing him over to the care of the Airl's physick, Reeve had decided to try his luck in the kitchens.

It had been many hours since his last meal in Cleeland, and his stomach had been telling him that a lifetime had passed. To his surprise, though, the kitchens had been deserted, and the only voices he'd heard had been coming from Lorimer's parlor . . .

After a few minutes eavesdropping outside the door, Reeve had the gist of the conversation, and he'd burst through it as soon as he'd heard the scuffle inside — almost, to his chagrin, too late.

Maven had, however, been pleased he had waited long enough to witness Lorimer's confession, and the Airl had certainly taken more notice of their story because there'd been two voices telling it. Lorimer had tried to deny the whole thing, accusing Maven and Reeve of attacking him, but Maven's assistance in helping to remove Lord Mallor from the castle had stood them in good stead.

Lorimer was currently cooling his heels in the dungeon below the castle while the Airl considered what to do with him. Sully's body had been removed from the side of the road by Myra, and buried with care and reverence on the day that he'd been found. But Maven and Reeve had decided to consult with Myra before raising Sully's murder with the Airl, so, at this stage, Lorimer was being held only for his attack on Maven.

And while all of this was going on, the Airl had reminded Reeve that he had failed to fulfill his mission — to find the Fire Star.

Looking down at his feet now, Reeve swayed a little at the enormity of the mess he was in. Despite everything that had happened, everything he'd done, his dream of being a knight remained in jeopardy.

He and Maven had managed to uncover a spy (Neale), unmask a murderer (Lorimer, even if he was yet to be judged for that) and even bring two unhappy people together in a happy union (Sir Garrick and Lady Cassandra). But Reeve would still be going home at the end of the day, and Maven was now even further trapped in her role as companion, and all because of one dazzling red stone.

". . . pronounce you man and wife . . ." the cleric announced with gusto. "You may now kiss the bride."

As Sir Garrick took his new bride in his arms, Reeve wondered if his own face looked as gloomy as Maven's did.

Around them, people cheered and clapped as Sir Garrick and Lady Cassandra embraced, their smiles tender. Reeve wondered at the difference a game of chess could make to one couple, but realized it was more about what the willingness and ability to play the game had shown each of them about the other that had seen them embrace the idea of their union.

As he followed the couple from the chapel, Reeve, with Maven by his side, tried to summon up a charming smile for the happy, excited people showering Sir Garrick and Lady Cassandra with tiny white flowers – honeysuckle, Reeve realized, breathing in the familiar, drifting scent.

Outside in the courtyard, it seemed that everyone in the surrounding country villages had come inside the castle walls for a glimpse of the bride. Reeve waved at Myra, who was standing slightly away from the crowd in the shadow of the chapel wall, and she grinned before bending down and hauling a man to his feet beside her.

Reeve almost laughed out loud as Kit lifted his ever-present cider jug in a toast to the happy couple. Grabbing Maven's hand, Reeve directed her gaze toward Kit and

Myra, and Maven laughed.

"I can't believe he still has cider in that jug," Reeve said, turning his attention back to Sir Garrick and Lady Cassandra, who'd stopped ahead of them to talk to a woman holding a baby.

To his surprise, Maven stopped short, holding up the line of people now trying to exit the chapel for the celebration feast in the Great Hall.

"Reeve," Maven said, resisting his efforts to drag her along. "Is that the jug that Sully gave him?"

Reeve frowned, looking across to where Kit was now tipping the jug up to his mouth, head thrown back, as though draining the very last drops.

"Well, I think so," Reeve said. "I don't think Myra would have a stash in her cottage."

"Reeve," Maven said, staring at him with huge eyes. "I know where the Fire Star is."

How could I have been so wrong? The jug lies smashed on the cobblestones, revealing nothing but a tiny dribble of cider inside. Stricken, I look to Reeve, trying to ignore the whispering of the people around us. When we had broken ranks from the wedding-party line to push our way through the crowd to Kit, they had muttered.

When Reeve had grabbed Kit's jug from him with a

mumbled sorry and then dashed it on the ground, they had protested.

And now, they just whispered.

"What is the meaning of this?" the Airl's voice booms from the chapel steps. Reeve looks at me, but I am unable to speak. My neck hurts, my heart aches and that feeling of exhaustion is once again overwhelming me.

I was so sure that the Fire Star would be hidden in the jug that Sully had left with Kit. My mother always said that I thought I was too smart for my own good. That people would always laugh at me and never like me for it. And, again, she is proven correct.

"I . . . we . . ." Reeve begins, and I watch as he draws himself together. "My lord, we thought —"

But now the Airl is barging through the crowd toward us, and I can see Lady Cassandra staring at me with questions in her eyes.

But Reeve has paused and is biting his lip.

He turns to me. "There were two jugs," Reeve says, his voice low. "Maven, there were two!" I can feel my hopes rising again as he turns to Kit.

"Kit, the other jug — Sully left two with you?"

Kit blinks. "Yes," he says, and I want to shake him to make him speak faster. The Airl is almost upon us, bristling with displeasure at the show we are creating at the special event.

"I finished the other one before I went to visit Myra,"

Kit says, looking perplexed. "So I left it behind."

I can barely breathe. "Where?" I ask. "Where did you leave it?"

But I do not need to hear his answer and neither does Reeve, for he is already moving toward the stables and I am a hair's breadth behind him.

The light inside is dim, but Reeve moves with certainty to the darkest stall in the furthest corner from the door. I start with the stall nearest to me, taking a moment to say hello to the huge inhabitant, who flicks her ears at me and whinnies softly as I peer over the gate.

I hear a scrabbling sound in the straw and then a triumphant "ha!" before Reeve emerges from his stall, a jug held over his head.

"Is it the one?" I am barely able to squeak the words out.

He does not answer, merely shaking the jug gently from side to side.

And I hear a comforting rattle.

"You do it," Reeve says, handing the jug to me. "I think Sully would like that it's you."

Testing the weight of the pottery crock in my hands, I give it one sharp, solid tap on the nearest beam, and a crack appears in the bottom of the vessel. One more sharp tap opens up a gaping hole, and I look to Reeve before tipping the jug, my hand under that hole.

With a slithering sound, it drops neatly from its dark

hiding place and into my waiting palm, where, smooth and cool, large as an egg, it flashes and winks at me as though lit from within.

The Fire Star.

CHAPTER TWENTY-TWO

"And so your future as a squire is determined, young Reeve." Sir Garrick was sprawled comfortably in the armchair in his chambers, looking like a contented man. To all intents and purposes, he was bathing ahead of the second part of the wedding celebrations. The pomp and ceremony of the official luncheon feast was over, and all those deemed not intimate enough for the evening's festivities had been dispatched.

It was the Airl who had decided who stayed and who went, removing anyone he suspected of being ears and eyes for the King, and Reeve knew that the real business of the wedding was about to begin.

"So it would seem, sire," Reeve said, feeling shy. "I trust that this meets with your approval."

Sir Garrick laughed. "It seems to me that Lady Rhoswen has once again proven that she knows best," he said. "I will never again question her decisions."

Reeve blushed, busying himself with pulling Sir Garrick's softest black boots from the chest. "These, sire?" he asked.

Sir Garrick looked them over. "Yes, I suspect these will be best — my Lady Cassandra will appreciate the softness of the leather as I trample all over her feet when we dance."

Reeve smiled, placing the boots on the floor and bending to help Sir Garrick ease the first one on. "You feel up to dancing, sire?"

"It will be a slow dance," said Sir Garrick with a wink as he tapped his well-strapped side. "But I would not miss it."

Judging by the way he winced as Reeve pulled the tight boot up to his knee, Reeve thought it might be a very slow dance indeed.

"Tell me, Reeve, how did you know where to find the stone?"

"It was not me who worked it out," Reeve confessed, still cuffing himself inwardly for not putting two and two together earlier. "It was Maven who realized first."

"Clever girl," Sir Garrick mused. "And lucky for, er,

Kit that you and the wyld woman were able to vouch that he was not the sweeping man, that you did not see him in the courtyard when the Fire Star disappeared, and that it could not have been he who had put the stone there in the first place . . ."

Reeve concentrated on straightening Sir Garrick's boot. "Yes, very lucky," he said.

"And Myra reports that she buried a poor stranger, answering the description of the sweeping man, who had been set upon on the Rennart Road," Sir Garrick pondered, though Reeve did not miss the probing beneath his words. "And so we have the Fire Star, and our suspected thief has met an unfortunate end."

Reeve proffered the second boot, hoping to distract the knight. "Yes, and I think Airl Buckthorn is happy to leave it at that."

"Indeed," said Sir Garrick, sliding his right foot into the boot. "As are a few other people, I suspect . . ."

"Come, sire, it is your wedding day," Reeve prompted, desperate to change the subject. "Your bride awaits."

"Speaking of my bride," said Sir Garrick with a bright smile. "Maven is responsible for Cassandra's prowess at chess?"

"I, er, well . . ." Reeve hesitated, not wanting to get Maven in trouble.

"Have no fear of me, Reeve," Sir Garrick said as he straightened the second boot. "I have never had a more welcome surprise than discovering that my bride-to-be could discuss more than the weather and her latest sampler. The secrets of that household are safe with me."

All of them? Reeve thought of the Beech Circle, but he would not mention that. Not today, not ever.

"It was she," he conceded.

Sir Garrick paused. "Airl Buckthorn wishes me to undertake a tour of some of our neighbors, near and far," he said. "It seems to me that if we were to travel with my new wife and her quiet companion, our visits would be seen as less . . . threatening . . . when viewed by others. What think you, Reeve?"

Reeve could not contain the beaming smile that crept over his face.

"If it pleases you, sire, then I can think of no reason that the ladies would not be of great assistance to your, er, diplomatic mission."

Sir Garrick stood up, smoothing his new tunic — still black, but now with a border of fine metallic silverwork.

"Neither can I, Reeve. Neither can I."

They look good together, both so strong and fine, her dark hair on his shoulder as they dance, turning in tiny circles to accommodate his injury. Now, he throws his head back and laughs at something she has said, and I can see the delight on my lady's face that he appreciates her comment.

It is not the freedom that I dreamed of, but I cannot find it in my heart to deny her the happiness she has now.

Talleben will wait for me. The Beech Circle will see that I get there. One day.

Sir Garrick spins her, and the Fire Star catches the light from the flickering candles on the table beside them. It is truly beautiful, flashing radiant prisms across the room.

I can see why Lorimer wanted it. It is just a stone, but it represents so much more: choices, freedom, social standing. Now, he can only dream of those things, lying in the dark on a stone bench far below us.

The idea that Lorimer will not pay the price for Sully's murder remains a thorn in my side. It is true that he will not see the light of day for many years, if ever, for trying to kill me, but it is not enough. Not when a good man died at his hands.

Reeve believes Lorimer will confess in good time. In Reeve's words: "He won't be able to help himself. Wait until he is brought before Airl Buckthorn next week to answer the charges against him and see if I'm not right."

Reeve then went into great detail about Lady Rhoswen and a footman who had been so desperate to prove how clever he was that he confessed to selling

Harding Manor's wine stores and covering his tracks by refilling empty bottles with beet water.

I cannot see the parallels myself, but Reeve believes that a vain, haughty beast like Lorimer will bring about his own demise. And if such a man, particularly one with huge gambling debts and a proven ability to act with violence, were to accuse Lady Cassandra of trying to engineer the disappearance of the Fire Star herself, who would believe him?

Perhaps even the intent to steal the stone for himself is enough to arouse the "pitiless bad luck" of the Fire Star myth for such a man.

We shall see.

Across the hall, sitting at the table just below the wedding party, Anice stares at Cassandra, and I know that it is the Fire Star that catches her eye. After tonight, it will become hers. It will be tucked away in a dark corner of the castle to keep it safe – her father's in name, but her dowry in nature. Hers.

I hate her a little for this. I can forgive her the meanness, the entitlement, the spite, but I cannot forgive that she will hold – even if in name only – the means to escape, and she will never use it.

I can only hope that Lady Cassandra impresses upon Anice – and Airl Buckthorn – the importance of tradition, of holding it for her youngest daughter, of the horrors of unending "pitiless bad luck." If black myths and rumors of sorcery are all we have as women to protect what is ours, then they must be preserved.

With a sigh, I turn back to my tumbler of ale, wondering what the morrow will bring. Tonight, I will tuck my lady into her new chambers with Sir Garrick, and wander back to my own sleeping mat in her former rooms. Tomorrow, I begin my new life, under the command of not just Lady Cassandra, but her husband.

I look up once more to find Anice's gaze upon me, and the malevolence in it makes me sit back in my chair. She does not like me. Few do, it is true, and that is something I wrestle with. I don't want to care.

But I do.

"Are you all right?" Reeve slides into the chair beside me, watching the Airl's daughter. Three tables down, Airl Buckthorn is sitting close with three men, all of whom have loosened their belts. He is speaking low, hard and fast, plotting under the cover of the lilting music.

"Fine," I say to Reeve.

"She hates you for helping her," Reeve says, perceptive as ever, still focused on Anice. "Because you glimpsed her while weak?"

I shake my head. "She hates me for not exploiting her weakness," I say. "She would have, had our roles been different. To her, it is I who is weak for not following up, for not demanding something of her."

Reeve sits back in his chair. "Why didn't you?" he asks. "You know how favors work as well as I do."

I laugh. "For just that reason. What I did in that garden was not a favor for her, but a considered move for myself and Lady Cassandra. I was not going to have that conceited girl and her scruffy admirer give the Airl an excuse to suspend the marriage that Cassandra needed at that point. And I have no desire, ever, to be beholden to Anice in any way."

I will not share with him the simple tenet of the Beech Circle, to help all girls and women always. He does not need to know.

Instead, we both consider the fair maiden, now gossiping intently behind a fan that does not quite hide her malicious glee.

"Good decision," Reeve says after a moment.

"The only decision," I say. "But now I am fighting a headache, and I am hoping the two lovebirds choose to retire soon."

It is Reeve's turn to snort as we watch Lady Cassandra and Sir Garrick on the dance floor. "You won't have long to wait. And Sir Garrick has given us a free day on the morrow."

I manage a smile at that. "I will go to Myra. She will have something to help my neck."

"I'll come," Reeve immediately says. "She has something for me, too. I was supposed to collect a tincture the other day but got . . . sidetracked."

I look at him curiously, but he says no more.

The music changes, and the space between the tables fills with whirling, clapping couples, driven on by the lively melody of the fiddle. Cassandra asks Sir Garrick a teasing question, and they retire from the dance floor, hand in hand.

"I hope you're ready to travel," Reeve says after a moment.

"Why? A lady doesn't travel. She stays in one place and awaits her lord's leisure. As does her companion."

He runs a hand through his hair, and I can almost see the blond curls that he had when I first met him on the road. I wonder how long they will take to grow back — or if Sir Garrick will allow it.

"Well, given that your lady will be traveling with me and Sir Garrick, you'll be going, too," he says with a smile. "Unless you'd rather stay here with Anice."

I gasp, both at the very idea and at the alternative he is posing. "You'd best explain."

"It seems that Sir Garrick feels that you will be of use on his next delicate mission," Reeve says, before adding, "Lord knows why."

I punch him on the arm but there is no menace in it, and I cannot suppress my grin.

"Does he indeed?" I say, looking over to where the knight is now whispering into the ear of a blushing

Cassandra.

"He does," says Reeve. "It seems that your knowledge of chess, not to mention the unearthing of the Fire Star, has impressed him greatly."

"Is that so?" I say, and I feel lighter inside than I have since I was ten years old, learning about the stars from my father.

"Indeed," says Reeve. "But —"

I wait. "But?"

"Well, it was when I told him about . . ."

I wait, on edge. Surely he hasn't mentioned the Beech Circle? Our network is not for the benefit of any man.

"About your superior goat-herding skills that he really came on board," Reeve says, dissolving into guffaws.

I can't help but laugh with Reeve, and, as we giggle on and the fiddle player spins into a wilder and wilder melody and the Airl mutters to his co-conspirators and my Lady Cassandra glows in the candlelight, I wonder if we are now friends.

I stop laughing as I turn the word "friend" over in my mind for, if truth be told, Reeve may be the first and only person that I have ever considered for this role. Cassandra and I have much that ties us, but, as I told Reeve that first day I met him, it never does to forget one's place.

But, as Reeve turns to me with a puzzled look, I realize

he has, through words and actions, proven himself a very good friend to me over the past few days. A strange feeling of joy floods through me, pushing the headache from my mind. "Let's dance," I say, suddenly jumping to my feet. "Give Anice something to gossip about."

With a half smile, Reeve grabs my hand and leads me through the tables toward a clearer space. Cassandra catches my eye and gives me a most unladylike wink, which I return.

My plans have not gone exactly as I'd hoped, but it seems that we have landed in an interesting place. With treason swirling around us, it may not be a safe landing, but we have each other, and, now, we have Sir Garrick, and we have Reeve.

And we have the Beech Circle.

It is all and nothing. Enough. For now.

ACKNOWLEDGEMENTS

Every book I write takes me on a whole new adventure – and not just a fictional one. It has taken so much hard work and several years to bring Maven and Reeve and the Kingdom of Cartreff to life in this novel, and I could not have done it without some wonderful people in our very real world.

Thank you to the wonderful and supportive team at Penguin Random House, particularly Zoe Walton, Mary Verney, Dot Tonkin, Tijana Aronson, Angela Duke, and everyone in the Marketing, Publicity and Sales teams. Special thanks to Joseph Mills from Blacksheep-UK for the sensational cover.

I am lucky to have my own Beech Circle and its branches are broad and numerous. Special thanks to those who walk with me along the winding writing path – Alex Brooks, Valerie Khoo, Allison Rushby, Megan Daley, Anna Spargo-Ryan, Sophie Hamley, Jacqueline Harvey,

Sue Whiting, Deborah Abela, Louise Park, Rachel Spratt, Belinda Murrell, Kelly Exeter, and so many more.

My extended family is large in number and loud on cheerleading, so thank you to Bev, Dennis, Bronwyn, Christine, Michael, Bart, Greg, Kate, Max, Noah, Ari, Declan, Lottie, Jake, Gemma, Elliot and Lois. Plus, Scout, world's best writing companion and goodest dog ever.

A huge and grateful thank you to the readers around the world for your letters, emails, reviews and photos. I hope you love Maven and Reeve as much as I do! Special gratitude to super reader Jasmine Sim of Jazzy's Bookshelf blog who read a very early draft of this book and gave me invaluable feedback.

As always saving the best for last, thanks and love to my boys — John, Joseph and Lucas. Here's to the next adventure!

ABOUT THE AUTHOR

Allison Tait (A.L. Tait) is the internationally published bestselling author of middle-grade adventure series *The Mapmaker Chronicles* and *The Ateban Cipher*. A multi-genre writer, teacher and speaker with many years' experience in magazines, newspapers and online publishing, Allison is the co-host of the top-rating So You Want To Be A Writer podcast. *The Fire Star: A Maven & Reeve Mystery* taps into her passion for historical fiction and adventure. Allison lives on the south coast of New South Wales with her family. Find out more about Allison at allisontait.com

ALSO BY A. L. TAIT

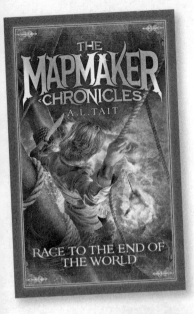

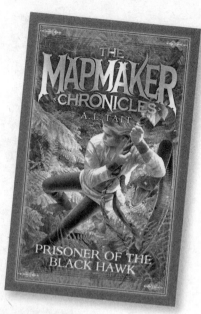

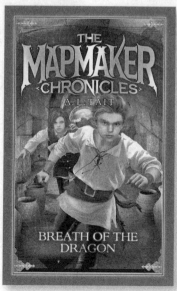

MORE BY A. L. TAIT

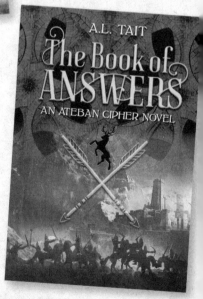